Cary and John

Neil Ellis Orts

D1127394

RESOURCE *Publications* · Eugene, Oregon

Resource Publications
A division of Wipf and Stock Publishers
199 W 8th Ave, Suite 3
Eugene, OR 97401

Cary and John
By Orts, Neil Ellis
Copyright©2014 by Orts, Neil Ellis
ISBN 13: 978-1-7252-5186-1
Publication date 9/16/2019
Previously published by Parsons Porch Books, 2014

Dedication

I'd like to dedicate this story to the memory of all the men and women who, in decades past, lived secret lives because they were thought to be dirty, perverted, or mentally ill, and also to the lives the secrets damaged.

Acknowledgements

Early readers and feedback is invaluable to any writer. I'd like to extend thanks to two of them. Lydia Hance of Frame Dance Productions (framedance.org) and the Rev. Lura N. Groen of Grace Lutheran Church, Houston (beinggrace.org) gave me invaluable comments and encouragement and I am very grateful for their time and insight.

Chapter 1

GLORIA ALWAYS STOPPED WHAT SHE WAS DOING at ten o'clock in the morning and prayed. She pulled one of the cushions off the sofa and placed it on the floor, at the armrest where there was no end table. There she kneeled, hands folded on the armrest, and she'd pray her morning prayers. Some prayers were always the same, for Fred, her husband, off at work, for her older son, Daniel and his wife, who was carrying Gloria's first grandchild, and for her younger son, Isaac, who hadn't made Gloria laugh in a long time. The prayer for Isaac was always the longest petition. She prayed for his return to the narrow way and to become the Godly man she raised him to be.

When she was a teacher, she would always pray first thing in the morning, of course, before going to the school. Once she retired—for which she always thanked God, everyday—she found ten o'clock to be early enough in the day for her morning prayers, but late enough that it gave her time to think about what was weighing on her heart. She was awake, able to come before the Lord in a more intentional way, with real concerns, not the repeated petitions she used to rush through while Fred showered.

Today, she prayed for Cathy, her life-long friend, coming over for lunch. They grew up together, next door to each other for many years. Both were the only child in their family and they grew up like sisters, or at least cousins. They called each other's parents "aunt" and "uncle." It seemed that Cathy was sometimes a little lax in her walk with the Lord, but Gloria had been through her own crises of life and faith, and Cathy had always been there for her.

She prayed for her church and the community closet she would help with tomorrow, sorting the donated clothes. She prayed for the Sunday school class she still taught, third graders, just like she'd taught at the public school, for the soldiers in Iraq and Afghanistan, especially those she'd heard about on the news that morning, brave young bodies wounded and dying. She prayed for their parents.

So much to pray for all the time, so much trouble in the world. When she felt that she'd said enough, she always made a point of kneeling still and silent, allowing the Lord time to give her a word or a sign. He seldom did, but she waited everyday, anyway. Those who wait upon the Lord shall run and not grow weary.

She got up, stiffly, but more easily than some people in their mid-fifties might. She patted the cushion back into place on the sofa. She went into the kitchen and pulled leftover baked chicken out of the refrigerator. She'd make chicken salad for lunch, like Momma made it. Cathy always loved Momma's chicken salad. This was the joy Gloria savored about having a lifelong friend. She knew what would delight Cathy and it was as simple as making lunch from leftovers.

August 19, 1970

Dear John,

I still haven't gotten a p.o. box. If you want me to write you at yours, I guess I will. It seems silly to me. Write to me at the house, if you want to write.

A month in, I feel like we have the new house set up. All the boxes are unpacked anyway. Gloria's bored. There's no other teenagers in our neighborhood. It'll be better when school starts. I hope she stops calling so much then, too. She misses Cathy, of course.

I don't know what else to say right now. Still settling in here, I guess.

-Cary

8- 25-70

Dear Cary,

We all miss you here. Sometimes I stand in the backyard and look at the fence between our backyards. Well, between my backyard and what used to be your backyard. I think about how excited our girls were when we first took it down. Cathy was talking about how small the backyard feels now. I said, yeah, it's half the size! Ha!

More seriously, Maddie told me she saw Cathy kicking the fence the other day. Maddie was worried she'd hurt her foot, but didn't intervene. She said Cathy needs to let out some of her frustration somewhere.

But if she breaks a foot, I'm sending you the doctor's bill! Ha!

One of these nights when Cathy calls Gloria or Gloria calls Cathy, I'm going to wrestle the phone away and ask for you. Do you think our daughters will let their dads talk a few minutes? Seems only fair since we're getting stuck with the phone bills!

Yours,
John

Chapter 2

GLORIA CHOPPED UP ONION. CATHY didn't mind bigger chunks of onion. When Isaac was at home, she had to put the onion through the food processor. He didn't notice the onion if it was pulped, but wouldn't eat anything that had recognizable pieces of it. Adults don't mind onion, they even like it, she thought. You have to sneak things like onion past children. Arrested development. That was the term. She was convinced Isaac suffered from arrested development. Something in him refused to grow up and become a man.

She acknowledged her part, of course. She was his mother. She and Fred clearly had failed in their efforts. There comes a point when a mother has to step aside, realizing her damage is done and she can't fix it, at least not yet. Maybe later, she could do more, but Isaac had to come to her now. He'd cut off meaningful communication. Gloria just had to turn him over to God, pray for him, and ask God's forgiveness for her failures as a mother.

The salad dressing jar was almost empty, so she paused to write it on her grocery list. The list hung on her refrigerator door, held there by a rock Isaac had painted at Bible camp years ago. Blue and white swirls represented the whole earth on a flat, round rock. Gloria never looked at that rock, hot-glued to a magnet, without praying for Isaac.

11

She kept such mementos of Isaac around, in view, to keep her in prayer for her son. She wondered if other mothers prayed for rebellious sons as much as she did. Surely they did, if they loved them as much as Gloria loved Isaac.

Every once in a while, she wondered if she loved him too much. She used to scoff at such a notion. "Too much love." It sounded like someone could have too much oxygen. But, Gloria realized, some people respond to overflowing love with gratitude and obedience. Others respond with rebellion. Did God love Satan too much? Surely, God never loves too little.

Gloria snapped her fingers. Cathy liked unsweetened tea. She put the sugar canister back in the cupboard but put the sugar bowl on the table, to sweeten her own tea. Cathy used to like sweet tea, but that changed after her college years. Gloria paused. Was her own taste for sweet tea a childhood thing, her own arrested development?

Well, they all used to drink sweet tea, all the adults. Gloria pulled the tea bags from the now cooled, darkened water. She poured the concentrated liquid into a large, glass pitcher and added water until it was full. It had been Momma's pitcher, and she smiled as she remembered the time she and Cathy used it to make their first batch of tea for everyone to share. They were no more than nine or ten. Cathy must have poured three cups of sugar into that tea. It was practically syrup. Oh, they were so proud to be big enough to help. Cathy poured the tea as Gloria held the glasses of ice, hardly spilling any at all. The adults, her parents and Cathy's parents, all took their first sips and Gloria and Cathy followed.

The mothers knit their brows and smacked their lips as they exchanged glances. Uncle John laughed and said something about having a little tea in his glass of sugar. The mothers looked away, to hide the laughter that was rising.

Only Daddy, always cool, encouraging, loving, only he kept a straight face and said, "Good work, girls," and took another drink. "Maybe next time you can go a little lighter on the sugar, but this sure hits the spot."

Gloria, doing her best to act grownup, said, "Do you think it's too sweet, Daddy? I like my tea a little sweet."

Uncle John said, "Glory Glory, this tea is a little sweet like the pope is a little Catholic!"

Aunt Maddie kicked him under the table, and said, "John!" But she said it while laughing.

Momma asked, "How much sugar did you use, anyway?"

Cathy said, "We just added sugar 'to taste,'" repeating the directions on the package.

Uncle John laughed harder, but Daddy, though smiling, said, "It's perfect, girls, just like you. A little less sugar next time would be okay, too."

"Perfect, just like you." Daddy always said things like that. Even when he had to discipline her from time to time, it was always with that message. He loved her and made her feel like she was the best thing on earth, or at least should try to be.

Was that too much love? And why did that instill in Gloria devotion and obedience when her love for Isaac brought about rebellion? Was it something Fred had done?

She didn't let that thought go very far. Fred loved his son, too. If Gloria had always been closer to Isaac than

13

Fred, she reminded herself that she was always closer to Daddy than to Momma. That didn't mean she didn't feel love for her mother. Gloria had been devoted to both her parents, and Gloria and Fred were both devoted to Daniel and Isaac.

Gloria shook her head and put the tea in the refrigerator. If there was a reason for everything, she might never know it. Maybe there was something to be learned in all this. Maybe the Lord was teaching her something. She hoped she might learn the lesson before Isaac was lost for all eternity.

September 2, 1970

Dear John,

Sorry I couldn't talk much the other night. Phyllis and Gloria were always in earshot.

Getting a p.o. box feels like I'm sneaking around. Like I wouldn't want Phyllis to see or hear something. At this point, what do you have to say to me you don't want Phyllis or Gloria to see? That's the point, right? To have secret correspondence?

We live over two hours apart now. We all miss each other now, but it'll be natural to grow apart sooner or later. Then what will we do with these p.o. boxes?

I'm sorry about the transfer. It was a hard decision. But everything is changed now. The p.o. boxes just seem like a way to delay the inevitable.

I'm sitting here now, realizing I'm saying things I wouldn't say in front of Maddie and Cathy. I guess I should allow you to do the same. OK, six months. I'll go get a p.o. box for six months. I'll let you know when I get it.

-Cary

9-5-70

Dear Cary,

Maddie and Cathy are asleep now. I could hardly wait to sit down and write to you! Thanks for calling with the box number!

I knew you'd come through! Ha! Why not? The girls have their "girl talk," I think it's fair for us "boys" to have a little private communication, too!

Man, it's eerie in the backyard now. The fence all patched up, your yard empty, all of Phyllis's potted plants, your lawn chair under the tree. You. All gone. You and your stupid promotion!

It's funny how it doesn't seem so eerie when we drive up. It just looks like Phyllis has pulled her plants in for the winter. The other day, Maddie and I were trying to remember the last time we went through the front door of that house. We couldn't! She said it's like we not only lost neighbors but also whole rooms that used to be connected to our backyard.

So I guess I should sue you for selling our spare rooms out from under us. Ha!

I'm hoping I can wean Cathy off the long distance calls before she breaks me. She mopes around a lot, missing Gloria.

But then, I mope around a lot, missing you. Maddie misses all of you, but she seems to carry on the best. The up side is that Cathy and I are getting all our favorite foods for dinner lately. Maddie's making them to cheer us up. It's not working, but it's still good eating! Ha!

I don't guess I'm saying anything much that I wouldn't say in front of Maddie or Cathy or Phyllis or Gloria, but it's nice to know I could!

Write soon. I can't wait to hear how miserable you are without me!

Yours,
John

September 30, 1970

Dear John,

We're settling in here. I guess we should, after nearly 3 months. Gloria had a new friend over the other day, so I guess she's going to be OK. She still calls Cathy every weekend. I guess I don't have to tell you that. At least we keep her to calling only when rates are cheaper.

Phyllis is getting involved with a women's group at church. She talks about getting a part time job. The other women in our neighborhood either work or keep to themselves. She's not making friends.

I guess I'm not either. I guess it's too much to ask to find new friends like you and Maddie. I guess that was a once in a lifetime thing, how we all got on.

A few men from this new job go out for happy hour two or three times a week. I've gone a couple of times. I don't feel like I fit in so well. Of course, you're the only close friend I had back there, but I guess you're different like me, too. I think this move was the right thing to do, but so far, it's kind of lonesome.

-Cary

Chapter 3

THE DOORBELL RANG JUST AS GLORIA was rinsing out a bowl. She was wet from elbow to fingertips and she wondered when she and Cathy started locking each other out of each other's homes. Decades ago, of course. It was only as little girls that they ran in and out of each other's homes as if they both belonged there.

Which, they did.

"Coming!" Gloria called. She carried a cup towel, drying her hands as she opened the door.

"Hey there, Glory Glory!" Cathy greeted Gloria with the nickname Uncle John had given her and Gloria responded in kind.

"Come on in, Cathy Cat." Cathy entered with her oversized shoulder bag swinging from the crook of one elbow. In the other arm, she cradled a Tupperware bowl. "What's that?" Gloria asked. "I'm making *you* lunch."

Cathy kept walking and set her bag on the sofa. "Mom went on a baking binge and gave me two bowls like this full of snicker doodles."

"Aunt Maddie's snicker doodles?"

"Yeah, I thought you might enjoy sharing the bounty."

"Oh, gimme!"

Cathy held the container away from Gloria. "Not until you've had a good lunch, young lady."

Gloria pulled her face into a pretend pout. "Well, since you called me young, I guess I can wait."

"That's my Gloria." Cathy led the way into the kitchen and set the cookies down on the counter. "So what do we have to eat to get to our just desserts?"

Gloria smiled as she pulled the chicken salad from the refrigerator, pulled off the tin foil that was covering it, and passed it under Cathy's nose. Cathy's eyes grew big. "Aunt Phyllis' chicken salad?"

"How fun is that?" Gloria said. "We made each other's favorites!" She set the bowl on the small table where she and Fred had breakfast, where she and Cathy often had lunch together.

"Don't give me any credit. The cookies are all Mom."

"I'll have to call her later and thank her. I can't remember when I last had Aunt Maddie's snicker doodles."

"Do that. I told her I was going to share with you and she went on about how she had to watch you when she made them when we were kids, how you'd steal the cookie dough behind her back."

"I'd still do it, too!"

"And she'd still slap your hand!"

"Well, I guess I come out ahead in this swap, though. You have to settle for my chicken salad. I never think mine tastes as good as Momma's. She had a special touch."

20

"Yours will do in a pinch, I assure you," Cathy helped set the table, as if she were in her own house. "You surely don't want to have my version of it again!"

"Now Cathy Cat, you need to let that picnic go," Gloria said. "That was ages ago."

"I've let it go, I'm just saying," Cathy said. "I mean, it was kind of late in life to be learning the difference between Miracle Whip and mayonnaise."

Gloria laughed. "And I still say it was all Fred's fault. If he'd just put it back in the cooler like a civilized man—"

"We might still have all gotten sick anyway!" Cathy shook her head at the memory. "I thought poor little Isaac would never quit throwing up."

"He did get the worst of it that day." They fell into the momentary silence that always passed through their conversation at the sound of Isaac's name. "Well, that was then," Gloria said. "We have a lot of good memories around this food, too. Let's sit down and make new ones."

A flicker of a knit brow passed over Cathy's eyes before she smiled and said, "Yes, well, let's eat!"

10-4-70

Dear Cary,

Am I a bad guy if I admit that I'm kind of glad you haven't found anyone like me there?

Cary, I'm not even trying to find another friend like you. You're not that far away from me—we'll see each other every few weeks, every couple of months, right? Not enough, not by a long shot, but some is better than none.

Our new neighbors moved in last week. You told me a younger couple bought it, you didn't tell me they had 3 small children! Yikes, but they're loud! And the parents either don't care that they have howling wild animals for children or they're too overwhelmed to discipline them. Cathy says she might get a babysitting job out of them now and then. I said not until she had her rabies shot! Ha!

But wow, that really makes your move real. Someone else is in your house! I won't mention what those little monsters have done to your beautiful backyard. In another century, I'd say they had a great future in pillaging villages.

I'm a little bit afraid for her life, but I'm actually encouraged that Cathy is talking about babysitting for the new neighbors. She tried to hide it, but I'm pretty sure she cried off and on the whole weekend they moved in.

And, okay, I did too, a little. Maddie didn't say anything, but she noticed. She looked at me, patted my cheek and then rolled her eyes. Ha! I had to laugh then, too. A grown man, crying over new neighbors moving into his best friend's old house. I think Maddie was worried she'd have to get a mop out if she let both Cathy and me get going.

But *I'm telling you, if these kids moved in next to you, you'd cry too! Ha!*

Maddie says I need to be more neighborly. She says, "Look at Cathy, even she's trying harder than you to be friendly." She's right, I'm being childish. I'm stamping my feet and saying, "I want my old neighbors!"

By the way, you never said how miserable you are without me.

Tell you what, you get transferred back to your old job and I'll do my best to convince these people to move out of your house. Deal?

Yours,
John
P.S. I'm not joking.

October 21, 1970

Dear John,

I suppose I've made everyone miserable.

Maybe not everyone. Gloria seems to be settling in. She's talking about some kids at school. I think she's been to one girl's house already. I expect to see an extra kid or two around here sooner or later. She likes her English teacher, complains about her biology teacher. I don't think she's miserable. I bought her a box of stationery so she can write to Cathy. It was a way to get her to keep the phone calls to weekend rates.

I found out happy hour is mandatory here. At least that's the only complaint I've had at work. My boss is a pretty good guy, I think. He just wants more camaraderie. He kept saying he missed me at happy hour until his tone of voice changed. I got it. So I go to happy hour once a week. I hope that's enough.

I don't know what else to tell you. I get up in the morning. I go to work. I go back to bed. In between, I eat breakfast and supper with Phyllis and Gloria. I don't spend as much time in the yard here. Maybe next spring.

-Cary

Chapter 4

I haven't seen Daniel or Allison for a couple of weeks. How's she doing?" Cathy asked as she made her sandwich.

"Oh, big as a house and needing to add on a room," Gloria said. "She's mostly in good humor about it, but I hope, for Daniel's sake, the doctor is wrong about the due date. Personally, I don't think she's going to make another month."

"I can hardly wait. It's almost like one of my own."

"I know."

"And since it's not, I'm insanely jealous!"

Gloria laughed. "Oh now, don't go getting jealous. You know you can hold that baby anytime I'm tired of doing it myself."

"Oh, you're cruel!"

They laughed like girls, like they always have. Gloria gave thanks for moments like these, ageless moments, women in late middle-age, still giggling after decades. She hated to admit it, but she doubted all kinds of things, but when laughing with Cathy, she knew there were things she could trust in the world. There was bedrock beneath the shifting sand.

"Aren't either of your girls seeing anyone?" Gloria asked.

"Oh, I think maybe Emily is, but you know her."
Cathy sipped her tea. "I'm never sure if she's seeing
someone until it ends in tears."

"She's such a pretty girl, it should end in a
honeymoon. Of course, that's another beginning."

"Well, what Emmy hasn't learned yet is that tears
come anyway, but it doesn't have to be an ending."

Gloria nodded knowingly. Cathy had her tears—
they both had, really, but Cathy had to decide between an
ending or continuing on. She and Charles seem to have
weathered his infidelity, but it was so rough for so long.
Gloria couldn't imagine. Could she have stayed with Fred?
She thanked the Lord once again that she hadn't been tested
in that way. Her own tests have been enough.

"And what about Amber?" Gloria asked.

"Oh, I don't need to even pretend she's going to
give me grandchildren anytime soon."

Gloria furrowed her brow. "What do you mean?"

Cathy waved off Gloria's look of concern as she
chewed. She swallowed and said, "Oh, nothing serious.
She's just such a homebody and bookworm. Emily has a
social life, but I don't think Amber does."

"Emily is the more outgoing."

"That's like saying the pope's more Catholic,"
Cathy said.

"Funny how two sisters could be so different."

"I'd like to add them up and split the difference."
Cathy shook her head. "It was kind of cute when they were
girls, but as young women . . . Well, let's just say Emily could
stand to be a bit more bookish and Amber could stand a
few nights on the town."

"I wouldn't worry about Amber. She'll come around." Gloria finished off her sandwich as an idea hit her. "Oh," she said with her mouth full and held up a finger. Washing it down with her tea, she finally said, "There's a nice young man at church. Craig or Greg or something. He's a good, studious type, too. Let me see what I can find out about him."

"Oh, Glory Glory, slow down. You know Amber would never go for a set up."

"I'll figure that out when I get there. Right now, I'm just going to research the situation."

"Well, it couldn't hurt, I guess."

"Nothing to lose. Don't you worry, Aunt Gloria's on the case!"

Cathy laughed, "God help us all."

"He always does, one way or another."

Gloria watched Cathy's face and saw something under her laughter. Decades together also give friends x-ray vision, she thought. Both knew when something was up with the other. Cathy had known when Gloria miscarried. Gloria had known when Cathy made her decision to stay with Charles. Neither said anything, both simply knew in the moment, the face beneath the face. But it was an unspoken rule between them. They saw but never let on until the other was ready to say it. It was as if they both needed time for preparation, to say and to hear. Of course, there were times, like now, when the specifics were cloudy, but whatever was on Cathy's mind, Gloria knew the time of preparation had begun.

"You know," Cathy said," Amber is still so close to Isaac."

Gloria smiled a closed mouth smile and nodded quickly.

"I tell her to bring him home with her, that I'd like to see him," Cathy continued.

"And what does she say to that?"

"She says she doesn't trust me. Maybe Isaac doesn't trust me. At any rate, the way she put it was that she wasn't going to be part of any talk show reunion."

"What does that mean?"

"She thinks that if she brings Isaac home, that I'll have you there waiting for them."

Gloria rolled her eyes. "Does she think we're so stupid to think that would work?"

"Apparently," Cathy said. She smiled weakly. "I guess she pretty well thinks everyone is dumber than she is. She's probably right, too."

"Well, I'm glad Isaac is still in touch with someone."

"And, well, I guess I'm glad she's going back to church."

Gloria arched an eyebrow. "I didn't know she'd stopped."

"She didn't want you to know. In her own egghead way, she is considerate of other people's feelings."

"Oh, that girl," Gloria said quietly. She had noticed that Amber had stopped talking so openly around her. This explained it.

"She's going to Isaac's church," Cathy said evenly.

"What?" Gloria knit her brow and leaned in. "You don't mean she's—"

"No, no," Cathy said, her hand waving away the thought. "She said she started just to support Isaac, but now she's thinking about joining."

"Really." Gloria shook her head. "Well, what do you think about all that?"

"I don't know," Cathy said. Her index finger traced the rim of her tea glass as she considered her words. "She said I should hear him preach, how I'd hardly recognize our quiet little Isaac. She says he's quite animated in his pulpit."

Gloria's voice had an edge in it. "You know that's not a real church."

"Well, maybe so," Cathy said, "but it's the closest Amber's been to one in over two years."

Gloria began to clear the lunch dishes. She realized she was starting to get angry when she should be sad. It wasn't enough to be rebellious himself, he had to go drag his childhood friend along.

She also realized, glancing at Cathy's face, that this was not the news Cathy was carrying under her laughter.

10-26-70

Dear Cary,

Well, what can I say? Sounds like we're all miserable and it's all your fault! Ha! Don't be so hard on yourself. You did what you thought was best and well, you're really not that far away. We just miss the day-to-day. I know I do. The holidays are coming up and Cathy is asking if she can spend part of the school break with you guys. I'll be glad to drive her over and pick her up. Maybe while I do that, you and I can find someplace to go and catch up, too.

I imagine it's harder on you guys there. Maddie has a few friends here, like always. Cathy goes to school with all the same kids, just without Gloria. But let's face it, if any of you were going to do well sooner than later, it was going to be Gloria. She's always getting involved in stuff, so she'll make friends. But Phyllis, well, you got to admit she's not the most outgoing person. If our girls hadn't lived next door to each other, I doubt Phyllis and Maddie would have become friends. Our girls really brought all of us together.

And me, well, you know, I pal around with everyone, but I can't imagine there'll ever be another quite like you.

So yeah, we're all miserable and lonesome and we all have you and your stupid promotion to blame. Ha! Seriously, let's plan on some time at Christmas and maybe later in spring we can plan a camping trip. You're not too far away to scrap that tradition!

Yours,
John

11-18-70

Dear Cary,

Sounds like our girls have the holidays all planned out for us, doesn't it? I'm glad it's working out to come spend a few days with you guys before New Year. It's especially nice to have an excuse for the in-laws to leave right after Christmas. Ha! I'm kidding, I love her folks, and it's just fun to make in-law jokes. We're seeing my folks for Thanksgiving this year, so that leaves you and Phyllis and Gloria for New Year's. I can't wait.

Time does march along, doesn't it? When you moved I thought, we'll see them before Christmas, it's not but a couple of hours. It's harder to do than I thought it would be!

Leave it to our girls to plan it all, work it all out. Now that they have, I'm really antsy to see you. All of you, of course, but you, the singular Cary, especially. Be prepared to be attacked with a big bear hug when we get there! Ha!

You know, I'll confess something. When I get your letters, I sniff them, see if I can pick up your scent on them. I swear I can sometimes. You can help me out by rubbing the letter all over you before you before you put it in the envelope. Ha! Why am I saying Ha? I think I'm a little serious!

I'm already plotting excuses for you and me to get away from the family for a couple of hours, hopefully more than once while we're there. I miss more than just the smell of you. I'd really like to get a taste, too!

There. I finally wrote something we definitely don't want the families to see!

Speaking of writing, do it more, will you? I know letter writing isn't your thing, exactly, and it's not like I stop at the post office every day to see if I have a letter from you, but I don't know, a couple of times a month? I don't even care what you write. Copy the local phone book if you can't think of anything. Just rub it on you before you put it in the envelope and I'll be happy!

Maddie says I'm less mopey lately. I think it's only because I'm excited that we have a plan to see each other soon. Cathy is marking off the days on her calendar until she gets to see Gloria again. If I could get away with it, I'd do the same. Instead, I just peak at Cathy's calendar now and then.

Have I mentioned I can't wait until New Year's?

Yours,
John

Chapter 5

Gloria opened Cathy's Tupperware bowl and offered the cookies first to her friend.

"Not right now," Cathy said. "I'm going to let lunch settle a little."

"Well, I've held out as long as I can," Gloria said. She took a cookie and bit into it. "Mm mm-mm!" Gloria's exaggerated bliss made Cathy laugh. "I'm taking one for the road," she said as she took another out, still holding the partial one, "but let's go get more comfortable in the living room."

Cathy followed Gloria into the living room. Gloria walked on to her easy chair but Cathy stopped to look at the picture wall, where Gloria had framed photos of both their families. They were there as little girls together, and then as adults with their own children. Cathy was standing in front of Gloria's favorite, one of the larger portraits, one of the last pictures taken before Momma died. Uncle John and Aunt Maddie divorced within the next year, so it was the last picture with all the parents together. In the center stood their fathers. Daddy, tall and broad but never fat, smiled in his reserved way. Then there was Uncle John, smiling broadly, always the more outgoing of the two men, the more loquacious. You could see from this picture who was louder. Uncle John had one arm around Daddy's waist, the other around Aunt Maddie's shoulders. Uncle John leaned forward, mouth open in a laugh. Daddy was taller and he had an elbow on Uncle John's shoulder, too reserved to put an arm around anyone but his wife, which he was doing in the picture. Momma rested her head on Daddy's shoulder, just like in so many other pictures Gloria had of them. Gloria had taken this picture herself, in front of her house. The whole family was there, Cathy and Charles, Fred, all their kids, elementary to high school aged. There were other pictures from that day, of the individual families and pictures of the kids, but this was the one Gloria blew up and framed for her picture wall. The fathers were both retired, and everyone looked so happy, so relaxed. Aunt Maddie was laughing, looking to the side, exasperated with Uncle John. Momma smiled tenderly, looking directly at the camera. She looked most at peace.

"Happy times," Gloria said.

"Yeah," Cathy said. "Isn't it funny? I mean, I marvel more and more as the years go by, how these four people, no blood relation between them, how they created this family. Us."

"We were blessed with something singular," Gloria said and she sat down in her easy chair. Cathy looked at the picture a bit longer.

Gloria wondered if Cathy was missing the happy times of her parents' marriage. That they divorced was a surprise to Gloria, to everyone, really. They always seemed so happy, happier, even than her own parents. Gloria always thought Aunt Maddie's explanation was non-sensical. "We love each other, Gloria, but we're not in love with each other, maybe never were."

But then Gloria had a secret she'd never told Cathy, one of the few she ever kept from her "sister." Once, years and years ago, while they were still in high school, but after Gloria's family had moved back to town, she overheard their mothers talking.

"Phyllis, what would you do if Cary had an affair?" Gloria had gasped and she knew she shouldn't listen any further, but couldn't help herself. She crossed the line from overhearing to eavesdropping.

"Oh, Maddie," Momma said in her soft voice," I just can't imagine it. I mean, Cary?" She chuckled softly.

Aunt Maddie said, "Well, maybe so."

"Really, he seems to have so little interest in, you know, S, E, X." Her mother whispered the letters. "I'm lucky I have Gloria to show for the trouble!" The women chuckled softly and Gloria had blushed at their frank talk.

"Well, I'm pretty sure John is, well, seeing someone."

"No!" Gloria's mother used the same stage whisper she'd used to spell sex.

"I confronted him with it. He didn't confess it, but he didn't deny it, either. He just said he was happy and wanted to remain a family with me and Cathy."

"Oh my."

The women had been silent a bit when Aunt Maddie said softly, "I think I even know who it is. Someone we know."

"Oh, Maddie! Who?"

Gloria stood so still it almost hurt as she strained to hear the women's conversation, but they said nothing for nearly a full minute.

35

"Oh, Phyllis, maybe I said too much. It seems ridiculous to me now. Forget I said anything."

Then the phone rang and Gloria had to tiptoe away quickly before she was caught.

But when Uncle John and Aunt Maddie divorced, Gloria couldn't help but think about that conversation. Had Uncle John been unfaithful? Gloria half expected Uncle John to suddenly appear with a girlfriend and get remarried right away. Even more surprising to Gloria was when Gerry moved to town and joined their church. Aunt Maddie took up with him and she was the one to remarry first. Uncle John never did, never even showed that he had another girlfriend.

Cathy studied other photos. Her face was thoughtful, serious. Gloria wondered if she should keep that photo up. Maybe it troubled Cathy to see her parents together and so happy, so shortly before they divorced. Gloria was glad her parents never divorced. She couldn't imagine either one ever remarrying, ever being with anyone else.

December 9, 1970

Dear John,

I hope you all had a good Thanksgiving. We had a pretty good trip up to Phyllis' mother. Gloria loves seeing her only grandparent, but I could tell she was getting bored by Sunday.

Sorry I don't write more. I sometimes try and then I don't know what to say.

It feels like forever since we moved. Then again, I still get lost in town. Or I think I want to go to a store or a restaurant and remember it's in another town.

We're all looking forward to the holidays. Phyllis' mother might still be here when you get here, but she's not staying until New Year's. It will be good to see you.

I don't know how we could get away from everyone. We'll have to see how it goes.

-Cary

12-15-70

Dear Cary,

Don't you worry about how we'll get away. Leave it to me! One night you'll take me to see your office and a bit of the town, you'll get lost and we'll end up in a motel the next town over. Ha!

I'm not kidding. I already called around. Found a place that charges by the hour!

Or else we'll send all the girls out to a mushy movie and we'll have the house to ourselves for a couple of hours.

Or maybe we can do both! Have I told you I miss you and I'm anxious to see you? Anxious doesn't begin to describe it. Ha!

Hey, Gloria and Cathy seem to be getting better at their letter writing. Maybe you could learn from Gloria. I'm just glad I finally got a phone bill I could pay in one installment!

Two weeks, Cary. Two weeks! Maddie makes fun of me and Cathy. She says she can't tell who is more excited to see you all, but she's looking forward to it, too. She talks about Phyllis almost as much as Cathy does about Gloria. I mean, we all know Phyllis is the better cook. Maddie misses having her to call when something goes wrong in the kitchen. Maddie is a good cook, of course, but Phyllis made her better. Maybe Phyllis can give her a few new tips or recipes on our trip. Cathy and I'd appreciate it!

Soon, Cary, soon!

Yours,
John

1-10-71

Dear Cary,

Happy New Year! Again! It was hard to leave you. I think Maddie and Cathy were more ready to come home than I was, but Cathy complained the whole drive back about how far away Gloria is now.

How good of the women to do all that after Christmas shopping, huh? How good to have all that time alone with you!

Let's plan something soon. We didn't go camping last year, so let's do that when the weather warms up a little. I'll check to see when the cabin is available.

You know, I try really hard to be happy for you and your new job. And your new house is great and all. But I still miss having you next door. Being with you again only made me realize how much.

I've asked Maddie how she feels about moving. She's not too keen on it. And I can't just transfer, I'd have to have a whole new job. It doesn't make sense to do that, I guess. But WOW, we need to get together more than every six months!

Write, will ya?

Again, Happy New Year! It could be happier, but it started really good!

Yours,
John

39

Chapter 6

"Oh Glory Glory," Cathy said and then said no more. Gloria couldn't see her face and leaned forward, elbows to her knees, the last half of a snicker doodle in her clasped hands.

"Cathy, why don't you come sit down?" Somewhere they learned to never ask a question that would result in a lie. No "what's wrong?" to be answered with "nothing."

"Isn't it funny how different things can be?" Cathy asked, turning. "I mean, all the appearances. You think you know how things are, but they're only appearances."

"We see through a veil. One day we'll see face to face."

Cathy made a face that she corrected quickly. Gloria knew it was either Cathy's dislike for scriptural responses—"trite," she called them—or else Cathy was about to tell a secret. Cathy sat down next to her big shoulder bag on the couch.

"It just becomes clearer after the fact," Cathy said. "It all makes sense, eventually. Mysteries you didn't even know existed get solved."

Gloria considered Cathy's words before speaking. "Do you think things weren't as happy as they appeared that day?"

40

"Oh, no," Cathy said. "That was such a good day, all of us together. Look at that picture. Uncle Cary and Aunt Phyllis so quiet but so—*loyal* to each other. Mom and Daddy, cutting up as always." Cathy smiled. "Do you know they were both over sometimes, after their divorce? You know, something for the girls or whatever. They laughed together just like in that picture, right up until the day Daddy dropped over dead."

"Well, that's what I never understood," Gloria said. "They always seemed so happy, got along so well." She finished off her cookie.

"They were," Cathy said. "To a large extent, they were. But, well, with hindsight . . . Cathy began to pick on a button on her blouse. "Well, I guess in retrospect I'd have to say they were more like college roommates who happened to raise a daughter together."

"Oh now, Cathy. What makes you say something like that?"

"My marriage isn't like that," Cathy said, and added before Gloria could say anything, "and neither is yours."

"Every marriage is different, Cathy. Every *person* is different."

"Of course," Cathy said and waved her hand. "But Gloria—I look at you and Fred and there's—what's the word? You know, not always but you can tell with people. You're not 'just friends' as we used to say in high school."

"Cathy Cat, you're talking in riddles today. We're *husband* and *wife.*"

"But there's more than just words to it with you. You're attracted to each other." Cathy looked away and said quickly, "I mean, you're *lovers.*"

41

Gloria blushed and giggled. "Well, yes, but I hope we're not staring wantonly across the room at each other!"

"Oh, nothing so obvious," Cathy said. "But—Oh Gloria, you know what I mean. You're the one who started the game back in high school!"

Gloria's face felt hot, but she couldn't help laughing. Back in those days, when they were high school girls remaining pure and chaste, they played an off-color game, guessing which couples they knew were or were not having sex regularly. It got to where they couldn't look at each other during church services if certain couples sat nearby, or else they'd dissolve into silent, quaking laughter. "Oh Cathy, stop!"

"Don't go getting all bashful about it now. How many times have I heard you talk about the importance of the marriage bed?"

"Well, yes, I do believe it is one of the greater gifts of marriage." Gloria tried to regain her composure.

"I mean, that couples retreat we went to that time?"

"Oh now, Pastor asked Fred and me to lead that session—"

"Because it's obvious you two are doing it!" Both women laughed. "With regularity!"

"Stop it!" Gloria's face was red from the laughter and embarrassment. She pulled herself together briefly and said demurely, "I'm simply a woman who takes her wifely duties seriously." And both women laughed again.

Cathy wiped at her eyes. "I was trying to have a serious conversation somewhere in here."

"Okay," Gloria said and touched her lips. "Serious again."

42

"All I'm saying is, I don't think our parents had that kind of relationship. They liked each other, even loved each other, but—"

"Oh, Cathy, what's wrong with you? No one likes to think about their parents and sex!"

Cathy smiled but her eyes drifted to the portrait. "I guess not, but it's a part of life."

Gloria rolled her eyes in fun. "As far as I'm concerned, it's enough that they had us. That's all the evidence I need on that subject." Gloria flashed on overhearing her mother speak of a sexless marriage, but pushed it away.

Cathy turned more serious and looked at her purse. "This is going to be harder than I thought."

"What?" Here, Gloria thought, is the heart of the matter.

"Gloria, I've been going through Daddy's things."

"Of course," Gloria said soberly. She knew the weight of the task.

"Daddy left a stack of letters."

February 3, 1971

Dear John,

A month has already passed. Sorry I haven't written. I start letters and then I get interrupted.

Phyllis and Gloria were so glad to see you all come and sad after you left. I wondered how Gloria would be. She's getting involved at school, making friends. I thought she might have moved on. When you left, she said, "I don't think I'll ever have another friend like Cathy."

I'm not sure about camping. I don't have any vacation time yet. I wouldn't be able to leave until after work on a Friday and I'd have to be back Sunday. Is just 2 nights worth it?

It was good to see you at New Year's.

-Cary

2-9-71

Dear Cary,

You make me crazy with waiting for a letter and then you write so little. Beggars can't be choosers, though. I take what I can get!

Yes, two nights with you is worth it! What are you talking about? Two hours with you is worth it!

I called up to the park. They have a cabin available the second weekend of March. I went ahead and reserved it, put down a deposit. I haven't said anything to Maddie, yet, but if you just can't I'll take her and Cathy up—they don't really like it, but since I already paid for it, they'll go. So save me from a weekend in the woods with two unhappy girls! Arrange it so you can go! Ha!

In fact, tell Phyllis and Gloria to come this far with you. They can stay with Maddie and Cathy and they'll have an all-girls weekend.

Look, I know it's not ideal, but you'll get off work at 5:00, right? Pick up your women and be on the road by 6:00, and you'll be here a little after 9:00. We'll be at the cabin easily by 11:00. So it'll be a little late. We won't have to get up early on Saturday. Or at all! Ha!

Maddie and Cathy have talked a lot about how much fun they had New Year's. I'm convinced we—you and me—had the best time of all.

Your letters are so reserved. I guess I hesitate to get too graphic myself. Is it too much to admit that just thinking about you—about New Year's and going camping—has me very excited right now? I'm so excited it hurts to keep sitting down! Ha!

Yours,
John

45

Chapter 7

L etters?"

Cathy reached into her bag and pulled out a packet of old envelopes, a rubber band around them. Gloria recognized Daddy's handwriting on the top envelope.

"You know, Gloria, I've thought of so many ways to do this. Now I can't remember what I decided was best."

Gloria was being infected by Cathy's nervousness. She prodded her friend. "That's Daddy's handwriting, there, on the top envelope."

"Yes," Cathy said, looking at it like she hadn't noticed before. Then she rolled her head around and put the packet of letters on the couch beside her. "You know, when you and your family moved away that time?"

"Of course," Gloria said.

"Right. Well, for those two years—"

"Eighteen months." Gloria knew how long it had been, almost exactly. She distinctly remembered ending her eighth grade year in tears because Daddy had taken a transfer to an office in another town, nearly two hundred miles away. She'd often mused at how close that town seems now, but back then, before she and Cathy could drive, before internet and cell phones, it may as well have been on the other end of the country. Everyone in both families shed tears when they finally drove away, never to be next door neighbors again. Gloria made friends in the other town, and really, it was there that she started taking her walk with the Lord seriously. In retrospect, Gloria thanked God for that year and a half, but at the time, she wasn't exactly filled with gratitude, not until Daddy announced he'd gotten a transfer back. If they'd been able to move back into their old house, everything would have been perfect, but by then, Gloria already knew life was full of blessings but almost never perfect.

"Well," Cathy said, "It turns out our fathers kept a correspondence with each other over those months." She looked up. "Did you know that?"

Gloria shrugged and raised her eyebrows. "No, I guess I didn't, but I'm not surprised."

"No, that's not surprising," Cathy said and let her gaze drift to the letters again. "They each rented post office boxes for it."

"Really? I wonder why."

"They wanted to keep their correspondence secret."

"Secret? Why would two friends keep a secret correspondence?"

"Oh Glory Glory." Cathy picked up the letters again. "Remember when Uncle Cary died, how Daddy cried?"

"He'd lost his best friend, of course he was upset."

"He was more upset than your father was when Aunt Phyllis died."

"I know, but Daddy was always such a stoic and Uncle John was such—well he was always more emotional.

47

More demonstrative." The two women paused, each searching for words. "I mean, look at us, we call each other's daddy 'uncle.' They were like brothers."

"That's what we said, wasn't it? 'Daddy's crying like he's burying his favorite brother.'" Cathy looked up at Gloria but couldn't hold the eye contact. "Actually, he was crying like he was burying his—spouse." She said the last word too softly to be heard clearly.

"What?"

"Gloria, this is going to upset you, I know, and I considered not telling you, not showing you, but then with Isaac—"

"What does Isaac have to do—?"

"I just thought he deserved to know—"

"Cathy," Gloria said, exasperated. "You're not making any sense. Just let me see the letters."

Cathy handed them over to Gloria, silently. Gloria took off the rubber band and tossed it on the coffee table.

"They're in chronological order," Cathy said. "The first ones won't tell you much."

Gloria glanced up at her friend as she opened the first letter. She read it quickly, furrowed her brow at the talk about the need for a p.o. box, but shrugged when she was done and left it out of the envelope as she opened the next one. Cathy sat quietly as Gloria scanned the first half dozen letters. "They're letters between friends," Gloria said.

"Here, let me see them." Cathy took the stack from Gloria and rifled down to a specific letter, from Uncle John. "Here. Read this one."

Gloria opened it and began reading. She knit her brow and then reread a passage over and over. She tried to find an innocent meaning to the words. They weren't graphic, but Gloria wasn't so naive as to not understand their meaning.

"Sweet Jesus," Gloria prayed, but could go no farther. She stood up and dropped the letter on the coffee table. She looked at Cathy, her friend's face full of concern, pity almost. Gloria turned away and for a moment, she didn't know where to go. The room tilted under her and she found her direction. She ran to the bathroom. There, she sank to her knees and vomited.

"Gloria?"

Gloria scuttled to the door and slammed it, locked it. She pulled herself up to her feet and leaned against the door, eyes closed, trying to fight a second wave of nausea. It was a lost battle. She made it to the bathtub and sat down. From there, she was close enough to the commode to lean over and vomit a second time.

She was in a nightmare, a sick nightmare. Chicken salad, snicker doodle, and bile. A very sick nightmare.

2-22-71

Dear Cary,

Why do you make me run up my phone bill? I just weaned Cathy down to a manageable level! Ha!

Ah well, glad we got the camping trip worked out. Cathy can't wait to see Gloria and have her spend the weekend. I think she's getting some other girls together for a party Saturday evening. I think Maddie's a little sorry Phyllis doesn't want to come, but we both understand. We hate seeing what the little hellions have done to your house every day! I mean, their house, of course. But we think of it still as your house. Luckily, it'll be dark when you get here. Only Gloria will have to see the place in daylight. I hope she's ready to see her old home in shambles! Ha!

I feel like I pushed you into this a little bit. I hope it's not too much of a burden. I know you have to do most of the driving. I went to this camp because it's the one we always went to. I didn't think further than that. Next time, I'll try to find something closer to you.

In the meantime, I promise to try extra hard to make it up to you.

Speaking of hard— Ha!

Yours,
John

March 3, 1971

Dear John,

If I'd known you were going to write smut to me, I would never have gotten a p.o. box. I guess I should have known that's why you wanted me to get one.

Yes, you railroaded me into this trip. Still, I can't help but admit I'm looking forward to it.

Believe me when I say I don't know what to do with you.

-Cary

3-15-71

Dear Cary,

 Something kind of funny happened when you dropped me off on Sunday night. It was while you and our girls were loading up your car. Maddie and I were alone in the kitchen.

 I hope you remember what I did for you on that county road where we stopped on the way home. I sure do! Ha! It made us late, but the weekend wasn't enough for me. I guess it wasn't for you, either. I have to say, your powers of recuperation are amazing!

 Anyway, Maddie apparently missed me. In those few moments we were alone, she attacked me! Grabbed my butt and kissed me on the mouth hard! I didn't have time to react, so I just kissed back. Well, it didn't last long. She didn't say anything, she just pulled back, one hand still on my butt, and she looked a little funny. I just smiled like an idiot and asked, "Miss me?" She smiled back, kind of recovered and purred, "Yeah" and tried to kiss me again. Then I remembered where we'd been all weekend, what we'd been doing and I sort of pushed her back and said, "Let me get cleaned up a little bit, I probably don't smell so good after a weekend in the woods." She just wrinkled her nose a bit and said, "Yeah, you could use a shower."

 Cary, I think she must have smelled you on my mustache. Or tasted you on my tongue! Although how the hell she'd know what that tasted like, I couldn't tell you! Ha! Anyway, after you and Gloria left and I showered up and Cathy went to her room, well, Maddie was lying in bed. She said she came down with a headache all of a sudden. I sat on the bed beside her and patted her back a little, said it was OK, did she need aspirin, all that. Meanwhile, I was kind of glad she lost interest because, well, I don't have your recuperative powers!

 I shouldn't laugh. I don't know if she really suspects what we were up to on our camping trip, but it was all kind of funny. I hope

I don't worry you with this, I just had to tell someone. Who else am I going to tell?

That was all just last night. I only told you good-bye last night and I already miss you. You and your damned job transfer! Can't they transfer you back?

Yours,
John

Chapter 8

G LORIA?" CATHY TAPPED ON THE BATHROOM door with her fingernails. "Gloria, are you okay?"

Gloria couldn't answer. She flushed the commode and pulled wads of toilet paper to wipe her mouth and then some more to wipe her eyes. She wanted to wash her face, but couldn't reach the sink from her seat on the tub. She didn't yet feel like standing up, not until she was sure the nausea had passed.

"Gloria?" Cathy tapped again. "Answer me or I'm going to go find Fred's tools and knock this door down!"

"I'm—" Gloria couldn't say "fine." She didn't have a name for what she was. "Give me a minute."

"Glory Glory, I'm so sorry," Cathy said to the door. "I should have known you'd take this hard but—"

"Give me a minute!" Gloria called again, louder.

For a moment, she couldn't remember why she was in the bathroom, feeling nauseous. For a brief moment, she thought, *this is ridiculous. Why am I throwing up?*

It didn't last. She knew. The letter. Uncle John, alluding to a disgusting act, one he thought Aunt Maddie tasted in his kiss! And her father. It was her father Aunt Maddie had tasted. She heaved again, but only a little slime came up. She had nothing left to vomit. She wanted to vomit it away, the whole disgusting image away.

There was that time, after they moved back, when Gloria and Cathy were sent to the store for ice cream. Their mothers were at a church meeting. Gloria had just gotten her driver's license. The teenaged girls had to turn back because they forgot the money Uncle John had set on the counter. They rushed in and Uncle John came out of his bedroom, asking what they were doing back so quickly. Cathy picked up the money from the counter and waved it at her daddy, giggling. "You'd forget your head!" Uncle John sounded more irritated than usual.

Then Gloria's father came out of the bathroom. "Back so soon?" he asked.

"They forgot the money," Uncle John said. Daddy laughed.

Gloria remembered her father wasn't wearing his shoes. That was normal at their house, but he had them off at Uncle John's and Aunt Maddie's. It seemed strange enough to notice, but not so much to mention. Now Gloria tried to picture where his shoes were. Were they in the living room? She didn't remember.

And those months away, when the families met for holidays and kept in touch with letters and phone calls. Gloria remembered her father's melancholy. When they moved back, how Uncle John embraced her father. Before the move even, the two men working in the yard, horsing around, the physicality of an elbow on a shoulder, an arm in the ribs, seemed so natural, so innocent. But after Momma died, Uncle John and Aunt Maddie divorced.

Her mind alternated between blocking out everything and giving into memories that now became tainted, lurid, and sickening.

55

She prayed quietly, "This can't be. Lord Jesus, this can't be."

"Gloria? Sweetie, let me in."

"A minute," Gloria called out. Then, more quietly, "Jesus, give me strength. Jesus, why is this happening? Lord Jesus, how can this be?"

Gloria took some deep breaths. Who was she? Was she this weak, sick girl in the bathroom? "Jesus give me strength. Be my help and strength." She was a woman of God, strong in the Lord. This was not—this could not be right. And if it was true, God would see her through this. God would not leave her in this shameful circumstance. There must be some redemption.

She made it to her feet and looked in the mirror. She washed her face and ran a brush through her hair. The words, in Uncle John's handwriting, tried to rise back to the front of her mind, but she pushed them away. She'd been weak to let them sicken her so. Was her Lord sickened by a whore? She would rely on the strength of the Lord, who would not be so sickened.

Not that Daddy and Uncle John were whores. She pushed that thought away, too.

Gloria unlocked the bathroom door and looked in Cathy's worried eyes. The nausea was gone.

"What have you brought into my house?" she asked.

March 31, 1971

Dear John,

I'm alone and have some time. I'm going to just write some things. You won't like them, but I need to get them out.

I'm always upset after we're together. Remorse, I guess. I don't think what we do together, the physical intimacy, is right. I always feel like we shouldn't have. I think it's a sin.

After four years of doing this, you'd think I would have said something before. I've wanted to. I didn't know how.

So I pursued this transfer to get away from you. I uprooted my whole family so I wouldn't see you every day. I thought after some time away, I'd start to feel different, but I don't.

Your last letter made me feel like I was really coming between you and Maddie. That for sure is a sin. Isn't it?

I've always been drawn to you. Even all those years before we became physical. I've never known what to do about it.

I want us to stop being physical. I don't know if that's possible. I thought this distance would help. It isn't. I'm still drawn to you.

I thought this would be a longer letter. I guess this is all I have to say.

-Cary

Chapter 9

THE TONE OF GLORIA'S VOICE MADE Cathy take two steps back. Gloria stepped closer again.

"How long have you had these letters? Where did you get them?"

Cathy sputtered before taking a breath. "Let's go sit down."

"Cathy! Where did you find these letters?"

"Gloria," Cathy said quietly and firmly. "I will tell you everything I know and I will talk all you want about them, but you will not stand there and shout at me."

Gloria's jaw flexed but she went back to the living room and stood in front of her chair. She looked at the letters on the coffee table, especially the ones with Daddy's handwriting, his familiar, careful cursive, envelopes addressed to Uncle John at an address she'd never seen before. She sat down and rested an elbow on the armrest, her forehead on her fist.

"Can I get you a glass of water? Tea?" Cathy became the hostess in Gloria's house.

"Water, please," Gloria said without looking up. Left alone some of the anger receded. "Sweet Jesus," she whispered and could pray no more words. She tried to imagine how the letters might be forged. Both had sent her notes and cards when she was at college, when she was at summer camp before that. She still had most of those notes, along with the notes her mother and Aunt Maddie had sent. She thought about getting out those notes and comparing the handwriting. She could surely find discrepancies. She could prove these letters Cathy had were forgeries, some cruel joke.

"Sweet Jesus," she whispered again. She didn't believe her own theory.

"Here you go, Glory Glory," Cathy said as she walked into the room and handed a glass of water to Gloria. One ice cube floated in the water, just enough to cool it, but not so cold Gloria couldn't swish it around to freshen her whole mouth. Cathy would think of something like that.

Gloria swallowed and said, "Don't say that right now."

"What?"

"This isn't a time for—girlish nicknames." Gloria took another sip from the glass.

"Maybe so." Cathy said and returned to the sofa. It passed through Gloria's mind that Cathy was sitting on the cushion she used for kneeling during her morning prayers.

"Tell me how you came across these letters," Gloria said.

"Well, you know, we cleaned out Daddy's apartment in a hurry," Cathy said. "He didn't have much anymore and what he had all fit in a U-Haul. We just loaded it all up and rented a storage unit. I've been going through stuff slowly, as I've been able. As I've felt up to it. You know."

Gloria nodded.

59

A couple of weeks ago, I stopped by the unit and grabbed a box. That's sort of how I'm doing it, a box at a time. These letters were in that box.

"A couple of weeks ago?"

"Well, yes." Cathy shifted in her seat. "I first read them a couple of weeks ago. Three weeks ago, actually." Gloria's face struggled between hurt and questioning. "I guess I had to sort of think about it myself a while, before I showed them to you. You know, *if* I showed them to you."

Gloria nodded.

"I didn't even show them to Charles. He knew I'd found something that upset me, but he didn't pry. I just let him think it was regular grieving.

"I debated a while, too, about showing them to you. I knew they'd upset you." Cathy smiled the smile she inherited from her father, the smile that always found something humorous in every serious thing. "I guess I should have showed them to you before lunch."

Gloria rolled her eyes and smiled despite herself. "I don't know I needed to see them," she said quietly.

"I know. But I didn't feel right keeping them from you." Cathy shifted again in her seat. "I was afraid I'd chicken out today."

"So you knew last week you'd tell me today?"

"I invited myself over to tell you." Cathy nodded. "I thought it would be better to tell you in your own home."

"I would have thought I'd rather hear bad news..." Gloria trailed off. "I guess. I don't know."

"I know, sweetie," Cathy said. "I know. For the first week, I wished Daddy and Uncle Cary had burned these letters. Then I became glad I knew. It explained some things. Not everything." The two women sat quietly a moment. "Some things." Cathy shifted yet again where she sat. "And, well, I sort of forced my own hand to tell you today. Before Isaac would call."

Gloria jumped at her son's name. "Isaac?"

Cathy spoke quietly and firmly, emotionlessly. "I sent Isaac copies of all these letters."

Gloria's mouth opened but no sound came out.

Cathy continued, "He should get them today or tomorrow."

4-5-71

Dear Cary,

Your last letter left me speechless. You're the only one who can do that to me, you know?

I mean—you moved your whole family to <u>get away from me</u>? You pursued this transfer to <u>get away from me</u>?

All those years, ever since we moved in next to you, I liked you. So quiet, so reserved, but I liked you. I guess I was drawn to you, too.

And no one was more surprised than me the first time you kissed me—and as I remember, <u>you</u> kissed first. Then after we were spent and you went back to your house, I worried the next couple of days, wondering if I was turning queer. I'd always sort of made fun of fags, you know? And I worried I was turning into one. I was kind of angry with you. Pissed off that you were making me into this homo faggot queer.

But you know, every time I saw you next door, over the yard fence—all I could think about was kissing you again. So the next time we were alone together, I did. I kissed you.

Now, since I got this letter, I'm trying to remember if you ever kissed first again.

Cary, I stopped thinking of us as faggots, stopped a long time ago. I think of us as such close friends that I can't imagine not being physical with you. I mean, they call sex making love, right? At the very least, there's some kind of emotional connection. Right? We're not just circle jerking here. This is more than just getting our rocks off.

Isn't it? I thought?

I'm speechless. I mean, I wrote some here, but I feel incoherent. Like I've been hit in the head. I don't know what to think.

Still yours,
John

April 14, 1971
Dear John,

You took my last letter better than I expected.

I know we have some real emotion between us. It's not the emotion that I have a problem with. It's the physical. The physical is pleasurable. I don't deny that. But is it right? You're a church man. Don't you feel guilty? We're unfaithful to our wives. We're crossing lines two men should never cross. It's just all so wrong.

A few nights ago, I was walking past Gloria's room and I heard her crying. I knocked on her door and asked if I could come in. She mumbled yes. She was on her knees, leaning against her bed, a pile of tissues in front of her. I asked her what was wrong. She said she was just overwhelmed with the goodness of God and what price Jesus paid for her sins. She said she was praying and it all just hit her, how her sins killed Jesus and how she wanted to be a better person. I tried to tell her she was a good person, but she just started crying harder. I knelt with her and held her until she stopped crying. I prayed with her, thanking God for her, that He gave me such a good daughter. I prayed for forgiveness of our sins and to help us all be better people. I guess other things, too.

Afterward, I couldn't make sense of it. Here's my sweet daughter, never gives us any trouble, and she is bawling her eyes out for her sins.

And here we are, you and me, just going on like we're immune to the wrath of God. What's wrong with us?

-Cary

4-20-71

Dear Cary,

You ask if I feel guilty. I guess I don't. No, I really don't. I don't think I even feel like I'm cheating on Maddie. I think I'd feel guilty if I were fooling around with a woman. That would be a slap in her face, thinking I could find a better woman than she is, because Maddie is a terrific woman. A good wife, a great mother to our Cathy.

But you, John, are not another woman. I knew that from the first time I saw you. Ha! And then I saw you naked. You are definitely, unmistakably, not a woman!

And I like that. <u>A lot.</u>

If I feel anything negative, it's that I didn't meet you first. That sounds awful, I guess. It's hard to imagine life without her, and I definitely can't regret having Cathy. But I run across an article now and then, about "gay liberation" groups in San Francisco or New York, and I can't help but wonder, you know? What if I'd met you first?

I've thought about what would happen if Maddie caught us. I can't imagine she'd kick me out. I bet once I explained it to her, how I'd never cheat on her with another woman, that you don't in anyway replace her, I think she'd understand. Maybe I'm crazy. (And I'm not asking your opinion! Ha!)

As for the church, I know they wouldn't look favorably on us. All I know is that I know what's good and I know what's bad. Being with you is <u>good.</u> I mean, I'm no minister, I haven't studied this, but if I may be so bold, I have to say—any God that doesn't like what we have going *isn't a good God. Being with you is good. God is good. All those people in the Bible had more than one wife and they weren't struck down for it. I can't imagine God is going to strike us down, either.*

Stop torturing yourself. There are murderers in the world. We're not so bad.

Yours,
John

p.s. It's been a couple of hours since I finished this letter and I got to say one more thing.

If Maddie did demand I make a choice, you or her— Cary, I'd choose you. We've been squeamish about this, always shying away from the word, but I'm putting it in writing here.

I love you.

And what we do in our private moments, however silly or ridiculous we get sometimes, is part of that love. It's pure. It's good. I've never felt dirty or "sinful" about it. I felt a little surprised the first couple of times, but I moved on quickly. I thought you had, too.

I'm nervous. I feel like you're trying to dump me. I'm not going to plead or anything, but I'm going to say this plainly. Please don't dump me.

I love you.

I'm yours,
John
p.p.s. I guess I got over being speechless.

Chapter 10

L ETTERS AND ISAAC.
Isaac went straight from Bible College into a non-denominational seminary. It was as he was finishing up seminary that Isaac sent a letter—not an email—home. Gloria knew right away a letter was something important. It meant he was buying himself some time between saying what had to be said and whatever reaction might come.

It was a very short letter.

Dear Mom,

I have decided to pursue ordination in the Metropolitan Community Church. If you don't know what that is, Google it. From there, you'll be able to deduce some things.

Love,
Isaac

And that's how Isaac came out to his mother. He was seeking ordination in this "gay church." Phone calls followed. And emails. A couple of tense holidays, over several months. Heated, pleading, grieving, hurtful, heartfelt calls, emails, and holidays, followed by silent estrangement. Cool birthday and Christmas cards, all signed "Love, Isaac" and "Love, Mom and Dad." Fred tried peacemaking, but he couldn't condone his son's actions either, even if he tried harder to overlook them.

But Gloria—a mother does not so easily give up her child to the fires of hell, especially not the child she thought she could not bear, not the child that brought her a laugh like Sarah's, not the child that had delighted her for a quarter century before he rebelled.

"Cathy, what have you done?" There was a volcanic energy beneath Gloria's question and she knew Cathy heard it.

"I thought Isaac would want to know—"

"You had no right!"

"Gloria—"

"Why are you conspiring with my child against me?"

"Conspire? That's rather extreme, Glory—"

"Answer me! How much contact are you having with Isaac? Are you and Amber siding with him? Are you all trying to go to hell?"

"Gloria—"

"You have to know he's going to throw these letters in my face, how this is some kind of *proof* that he was born that way!"

"Well, maybe—"

"It's not enough that you have to upset me with this—this—question of Daddy's salvation."

"Glo—"

"You have to use it to turn my son further away from God!"

"Stop it Gloria!" Cathy seldom raised her voice. It was enough to make Gloria pause. "Deep breaths, Gloria. Breathe."

"Oh, Cathy." Gloria lowered her forehead to her fist again.

"No one here is against you. No one here is against God."

"But it's *all* against God," Gloria said.

"Maybe so," Cathy said and sank back into the couch. "Or maybe not. I don't think I can tell most days."

"That's because you don't spend enough time in the Word, Cathy. I've told you time and again."

"Yes, you have."

"Don't worry, Cathy Cat," Gloria said, trying to lighten her tone if only a little. "I'm not up for a biblical argument just now."

"I can say a 'praise the Lord' to that."

Gloria looked up. "After Momma died—this is why your parents divorced!" Cathy nodded. "Aunt Maddie said, 'We love each other, we're just not in love.'"

"Yeah," Cathy said quietly. "When I found these letters, I talked to Mom about them."

"Aunt Maddie knows about the letters?"

"She didn't until I told her about them. But she knew about Daddy and Uncle Cary."

Gloria thought back to her teenaged eavesdropping. Aunt Maddie suspected as far back as then. Momma couldn't imagine it.

After a silence, Cathy continued. "Mom said as long as Aunt Phyllis was alive, she could bear it. Once your mom was dead, though, she just felt in the way. A third wheel."

Gloria put her head in both her hands as the length of the affair sank in. "And Gloria, Mom says being married to a man who actually wants her, you know is attracted to her physically, she says it's so different. She loved my daddy, she says, and she knows he loved her. But it's only now that she feels desired."

"Oh, Cathy, stop!"

Cathy sat quietly as Gloria tried to hold back from crying.

"Momma," Gloria said. "Poor Momma. She never knew."

"No," Cathy answered. "Mom says she doesn't think Aunt Phyllis ever knew."

"Not that! Momma— Daddy didn't—." Gloria looked to Cathy. "They loved each other but they weren't in love?"

Gloria began to sob.

April 28, 1971

Dear John,

I feel the same way. About you, I mean. I still feel guilty. I still feel like I'm cheating on Phyllis. I worry how all this would hurt Gloria if she found out. But I feel the same way about you.

I just don't know what to do about it. It doesn't seem to fit in with God's will.

But I feel the same way about you. If I didn't, I would have just walked away and not looked back. If I didn't, we wouldn't be writing these letters.

It feels like we met too late in our lives. I don't know what to do about that, either.

-Cary

5-4-71

Dear Cary,

    You feel the same way about me and yet you feel bad.
    Well, buddy, I hate to tell you, but maybe you don't feel the same way about me as I do about you.
    Because I feel good about you.
    Okay, I don't feel so good about you moving to another city to get away from me. That makes me feel bad. So maybe we do feel some similar things.
    Can't we feel more good than bad?

Yours,
John

Chapter 11

MOMMA WAS A VERY QUIET WOMAN, quieter even than her husband. She could be a little playful with Aunt Maddie, but then that was Aunt Maddie's nature. Aunt Maddie and Uncle John, both, were always joking, chattering.

One day, before the time away, both families were all in the backyard. It was after they'd removed a section of the fence between their yards and Gloria and Cathy were running back and forth. Gloria didn't remember it being any special occasion. Maybe they were all just working in their yards. Uncle John and Daddy both loved working in their yards, Uncle John more of a tree and shrub man, Daddy planting perennials and nursing rose bushes. Uncle John was out in his undershirt, dark hair all over any exposed skin, so exhibitionist compared to her own father's work shirt, on which he might unbutton two buttons if it were an especially hot day. Aunt Maddie questioned every landscaping decision Uncle John made, his only answer being laughter and a hearty, "Trust me!" Aunt Maddie would slap his hairy arm, he'd throw leaves or dirt at her blouse, laughing, always laughing, Gloria remembered. How they loved each other, she thought. *But not in love.*

Her own parents' yard keeping seemed delicate in comparison. Her father mowed the grass, her mother carefully lined up the young marigolds or zinnias, whatever her father had picked out for that year. It seemed sometimes that Momma and Daddy viewed Uncle John and Aunt Maddie as their own personal sitcom, enjoying their neighbors' shenanigans and glad for a playmate for their daughter.

This one day, though, after the antics between Aunt Maddie and Uncle John died down, Daddy was next to Uncle John, the standing portion of the yard fence in between.

"You two are something else," Daddy said, shaking his head.

"Ah, we just have fun," Uncle John said. "You two should try it sometime."

Daddy raised his eyebrows briefly. "I guess we just have more subtle fun."

"Subtle? Is that what you call it?"

"Quieter?" Daddy smiled.

Gloria knew they were joking, even if she didn't know exactly what "subtle" meant. Over the years, she mused how she and Cathy were learning things from both sets of parents. Gloria became more outgoing because she so enjoyed Cathy's parents. Cathy could sometimes be more "subtle" in mood because Gloria's parents modeled that for her.

"Definitely quieter," Uncle John said. "Sometimes I wonder if we'd be friends if it weren't for our daughters."

Daddy looked Gloria in the eyes and said, "I am always thankful for my Gloria." Then he looked Uncle John in the eye. "And if our daughters are the reason we're friends that makes me doubly thankful."

Then her father, the taller of the two men, reached across the fence and placed his hand on the base of Uncle John's neck, in the spot between his neat haircut and the exposed patch of hair on his back, where his undershirt dipped down. She saw her father's hand give Uncle John a slight squeeze.

Gloria always held that memory dear, the way Daddy expressed his thanks for her, how he loved her, how loved she felt. She also remembered feeling the affection between the two men, how proud she was to help Daddy make a friend.

Momma broke the moment. Quiet as she was, she was also quietly physical. Gloria felt her mother's hand lightly cup the back of her head as she walked by. "What are you boys up to?" she asked as she slipped an arm around her husband's waist and laid her head on his chest. She was the perfect height for that. It was how they posed in most of the pictures Gloria had of them.

"Doesn't he stink?" Uncle John asked.

Momma wrinkled her nose and said, "A little, but it's okay."

Gloria thought again, how they love each other. *But not in love.*

Cathy patted Gloria on the shoulder, bringing her into the present. "Gloria, here, have a tissue or two."

Cathy held a box of tissues. Gloria pulled out three, wiping her face, still crying, but not sobbing any longer. She blew her nose.

All that love in that backyard, all those people loving one another, real affection.

But no one in love but their fathers.

75

May 26, 1971

Dear John,

Weird thing happened. I can't tell anyone else about it.

Last week, I'd gotten behind in some work. We all have keys to the place, so it's not a big deal to stay late a night or two to catch up.

I worked for over an hour and then got up to go to the men's room. The building felt empty. You know, deserted. The men's room is shared by the whole floor and down the hall from my office. I was surprised when another man came in but just figured it was another late worker. I didn't recognize him. He may have even been from another floor, for all I know, another company even. He came in and stood at the urinal next to mine. He was young, or at least compared to me. Around 30, I guess.

You know how we talked about how we used to glance sideways at urinals, catch a glimpse? I guess I still do it. This guy caught me. I did the sideways glance and I saw he was watching my face. He grinned at me. I zipped up to get away.

But when I turned, he put a hand on my shoulder. When I faced him, he was pulling on himself, just hanging out of his fly. He was aroused.

I didn't know what to do or say. Then he put one hand on me, started groping me. I couldn't move. Neither of us said anything.

I don't know what I would have done if another guy hadn't walked in. The urinals are shielded from the door, so we had time to break apart. I wanted to run, but somehow, I had the presence of mind to stop to wash my hands. I knew it would be more suspicious to run out the door. I was much cooler than I felt.

I guess the young guy turned back to the urinal to zip up. I turned off the water as he approached the sink. I looked up in the mirror and he winked at me. The third guy had gone into a stall. That's when I ran. Walked quickly. I got out of there. I was afraid the younger guy would follow me. I didn't even go into my office. I locked the door and ran to the stairs, ran down to my car. I drove off as quickly as I could. I had to pull into an empty parking lot to catch my breath. Calm down.

I've never had anything like that happen before. Have you? I haven't seen the guy since. I still guess he works somewhere in the building. I don't know how else he got in.

It shook me up, I guess. Just had to tell someone. It's not the sort of thing I tell Phyllis. I've never even heard of such a thing happening.

Not much else going on here. Everything else is normal, compared to this.

-Cary

6-3-11

Dear Cary,

Hey, I guess that's kind of wild, what you say happened there in the men's room. I've heard of such things, but they've never happened to me.

What I don't like is how you just stood there. Cary, next time some bathroom fag grabs you, first you slap his hand away and, second, you punch him in the face! I'm serious. I know nothing happened this time, but it sounds like it might have if not for the third guy walking in. That bothers me, Cary. It bothers me a lot.

Look, I've never cheated on Maddie with another woman and I've never cheated on you with another man. I never considered it and never thought you'd cheat on me. Now, I don't know.

I guess we've never talked about it, but I'm talking about it now. Promise me you won't play around with another man. If you did, it would break my heart. And make me mad as hell.

Please, Cary, promise me. Send me a letter promising me.

I promise to be true to you.

Love,
John

Chapter 12

GLORIA STOOD UP TOO QUICKLY. Her empty stomach and crying made her lightheaded so she swayed slightly. She caught herself, though. She was not going to be knocked down by this.

Gloria turned to her picture wall and took the few steps to it. She studied the images as if they were all new.

"Lies," she said softly. Cathy heard her but didn't react. "All these pictures. They say the camera doesn't lie, but these . . ."

"They're not lies."

"Then what are these?" Gloria looked from photo to photo, looking for something familiar. "I don't see much truth anywhere."

"Maybe so," Cathy said, sighing. "But Gloria, I looked at my photos, too, all my albums. I wanted to see, too, see if what I remembered was still there. And you know, it is, it's all like I remembered. I just know more now. I see more now."

"They're all tainted," Gloria said.

Cathy pointed at one. "Even this one?"

Gloria looked at her and Fred on their wedding day. "I hope not," she said softly.

"How about this one?"

Gloria as a teenager clung to Daddy's neck, he smiling, almost apologetically, as if the intense love of his daughter embarrassed him. "I remember that day," Gloria said. "Daddy said to me, 'Gloria, your old man has some regrets in his life, but I'll never regret having you as my daughter.'"

"When you read the letters, you'll see how often he speaks of you. He loved you, Gloria. That is true."

"I always wondered what he regretted," Gloria said "What would my wonderful daddy have to regret? Now I look at that picture and wonder—did he regret cheating on Momma? Did he regret ever marrying her? But how could he regret marrying her and not regret me?"

Cathy shook her head and turned away.

"And here," Gloria said pointing again at her wedding portrait. "You know what he said, over and over during our engagement? Even on my wedding day? He asked me, over and over, 'Are you in love with Fred? Are you sure he's in love with you?' All these years, I thought he was just being protective of me, making sure his little girl's heart was okay. Now I wonder what else was behind his question. 'Because Gloria, I'm not in love with your mother and I regret marrying her.'"

Cathy smiled despite the situation. "You still mimic Uncle Cary perfectly."

"I'm not trying to be funny."

"I know."

"It's all tainted," Gloria said. "All these photos, they're all veneer over hidden wickedness."

Cathy flinched. "Wickedness?"

"What do you call cheating on your wives?"

Cathy didn't respond.

Gloria went on. "And a homosexual affair at that."

"They were our fathers."

"I can't excuse sin just because they're our fathers!"

"Can you forgive them?"

Gloria snapped her head toward Cathy. "Forgiveness follows repentance. Did they ever repent?"

Cathy sighed and slumped onto the couch. "It sounds like it was pretty well until death did them part."

"Don't mock the marriage vows with this abomination!"

"Glory Glory, you're starting to slip into caricature."

Gloria pursed her lips and turned back to her photo wall. She looked again at that picture of their parents, all four together. Uncle John laughing like he was delighting in his sin. Aunt Maddie also laughing, in on the joke, exasperated by it, laughing her only defense. Momma, the only innocent in the picture, resting her head on the man who regretted marrying her. Daddy, who never regretted having a daughter, but suddenly looked ashamed of everything else.

Everything had changed. Everything was tainted.

June 23, 1971

Dear John,

I'm sorry. I was thoughtless. I thought it was a weird experience. Funny even. I didn't consider how you'd feel about it.

We've never made any promises. I think it's always been understood. To some extent, anyway. I never considered any other men. I don't know what to do with you! I moved my family to a whole other city to try to stop carrying on with you. I can't imagine trying to take on another.

I was so surprised by that guy in the men's room. I don't know his intentions. I don't know how far I would have let him go. I haven't seen him since. I don't know who he was or how he got in after hours.

I'll tell you the whole truth. I always thought I simply wasn't that interested in sex. Phyllis and I are not that regular, I guess you'd say. I think she's more interested than I am. She's more often the one to start. Most of the time, I can't finish what she started, if you know what I mean. When I'm with you that never seems to be a problem.

Sometimes, I almost ache to be with you. It's sort of like I remember being a teenager, except it's different from just being horny. Like a teenager, I take care of myself. In the bathroom at home, while Phyllis and Cathy are asleep, late at night. A man my age, like a teenager in the bathroom, late at night.

I guess all you have to be jealous of is my right hand.

I can't believe I'm writing this. Burn this letter after you've read it.

All I really meant to say is I'm sorry I upset you. I never meant to.

-Cary

7-2-71

Dear Cary,

Maybe I overreacted. I don't know. I'm really more upset that you orchestrated this move to get away from me. Imagine how that feels to me. You leave to get away from me, then I get a letter telling me about another man touching you.

You might say it pissed me off a little.

I'm writing now with a cooler head and I'm sorry for whatever I may have said when I wasn't so cool.

I don't know where we stand, but I'll tell you what I feel.

I love you. We've avoided saying that, but I think we need to say it. Admit it. Or I need to admit it, say it clear. I love you and I don't know what that means now. When you got the transfer, I thought, ok, this is good for you and not that far away. But now you say you pursued that transfer, to get away from me. I don't know what to say about that.

You know, I love Maddie, have a great time with her. You see us. We're always laughing. That's how we are in bed, too. Laughing, silly. Crazy Maddie and John.

With you, I learned what the love songs are about. I learned what making love meant. We have our laughs, right? We have fun. But it's different with you, more sincere, I guess. When I hear love songs on the radio, I think of you.

Here lately, though, I think of you when I hear the break up songs, too. The "he left me" songs. The broken heart songs.

I'm sorry. I don't know where we stand. Still, I'm determined to sign my letters to you:

Love,
John

July 28, 1971

Dear John,

The days are getting away from me. Summers are supposed to be lazy days. I'm busy at work and I'm busy at home. We're putting in some work into the yard. It's nothing like what we did when were next door to you, but it's time consuming. Phyllis put in a small flower bed and then dug up a patch for a few vegetables. I swear there are more weeds here than there were there. We're having a time keeping ahead of them.

I think Gloria has a boyfriend. She's not saying as much, and Phyllis has asked, but she's certainly hanging around a boy from church. Nice enough kid. We don't object to it. I guess she's the right age for crushes like that. I don't like how it reminds me how old I am.

Phyllis is working part time at a flower shop. I don't know how long she'll do it. We don't need the money and she's not enjoying it a whole lot. She was hoping to meet people, make a friend or two. It's funny to watch my girls. Gloria is missing Cathy less, making friends. Phyllis is missing Maddie more. I guess neither of us is making friends here like we had with you and Maddie.

Well, that's the news here. I hope you're all doing ok.

Your faithful friend,
-Cary

8-3-71

Dear Cary,

I was glad to hear from you, but I've got to ask. What the hell kind of letter was that? We're having serious correspondence and then I don't hear from you for a month. I was hoping for a little more than a garden report.

But, okay, glad to know everything's going swell there. Don't tell Cathy that Gloria is moving on to other friends, though. You and I know it's natural, but Cathy still tells everyone Gloria is her best friend.

We've kind of let our yard go this year. We're just doing minimal maintenance. We don't like the new neighbors enough to risk seeing them in the yard.

Cathy misses Gloria, Phyllis misses Maddie more, not less. In a race for misery, though, I declare myself the winner. I miss you most of all and I don't know where we stand.

Love,
John

August 18, 1971

Dear John,

I was only trying to write a more normal letter. What do normal men write to their friends? I guess we're just not normal. I shouldn't try.

I looked again at your last couple of letters. You want to know where we stand. I honestly don't know how to answer that. It seems this last year I've created some misery for our families. Seems like I should do something to correct that. Make amends. If I could get comfortable with our affair, I suppose that would solve a lot. I guess if it was just you and me, well, I don't know if that would make it easier or not. Easier to carry on with you because I wouldn't be cheating on Phyllis or easier to just cut ties and try to live a life as a normal man. I can't guess. Since we both have families, and they're all so close—well, it seems like that's what makes it harder to carry on with you and harder to stop. Could our families remain so close and you and I be "just friends?" (That's what Gloria told that boy at church. They are "just friends," not dating. I'm not sure even she believes it.)

My office isn't very far from the university campus here. I go to their library sometimes, after work. I tell Phyllis I go there, that I'm reading Time and Newsweek there, rather than subscribing or buying them at the store. What I'm doing, though, is looking up books on homosexuality. There's not many there. Most of the time, I have to find books on sex and find the chapter on "sexual abnormalities" or something like that. The newer the book, the more it tries to make it sound normal, but most still don't have much good to say about it. And when I try to find religious books about it, forget it. I came across an article about a homosexual church once, but it didn't sound very convincing to me.

Just speaking for myself, here's where I stand. I want to be a good Christian. I want to be a good Christian father to Gloria, a good Christian husband to Phyllis. I want to be your friend. I even want to be more than "just friends" with you. I feel like I'm failing at all of the above. Try as I might, I'm failing. John, I don't want to race you in this, but right now I'm feeling like I could give you a run for your money on misery.

I wish I could tell you where we stand. Personally, my feet keep flying out from under me.

Your faithful friend,
Cary

8-24-71

Dear Cary,

I guess its good you're reading and researching in the library. It makes me smile, laugh even. It's so like you.

You know what I like most about our private moments? In those moments, I see you. I see your emotion. You stop thinking and I see you feeling.

You're not going to find me in the library. You're not going to find <u>us</u> in a book.

What about <u>us</u>? Do we have to fit between the covers of a book for you to feel good about us?

I started to make a joke about feeling good between the bed covers, but it didn't seem all that funny.

Love,
John

August 25, 1971

Dear John,

I've tried and I can't write down what I'm going to do. I guess I don't have to. You'll know.

What I have to say now is, I'm sorry. I wish I could keep on but it's too hard. I don't know any other way to stop.

Tell Maddie and Cathy I loved them. I loved you. All of you.

-Cary

Chapter 13

YOU KNOW, GLORIA," CATHY SAID but then paused. Gloria knew the tone. She did not turn around.

"What if," Cathy said and paused again, pulling herself forward so she sat on the edge of the sofa. She rested her elbows on her knees. "Just—what if the real marriage was between our fathers and what they had with our mothers was the sin?"

"Oh, Cathy." Gloria lowered her head, disappointed with her friend. "Don't start with that twisted logic. You're above that."

"Maybe so," Cathy said. "I should say, I was upset when I read the letters, too. I was angry for our mothers. I was so very pissed off at Daddy. You know, Charles and all."

"Charles has repented and tried to make amends."

"Maybe so." Cathy sighed. "Gloria, just read the letters. Sit with them for a couple of weeks, like I have."

"I don't know that I can. You saw how I reacted to what I already read."

"I've never known you to be so squeamish."

"I've never been confronted with the image—I can't say it."

"It's all right. I'm not so comfortable discussing some details myself. But Gloria, read the letters. They were in love. It wasn't always easy, there's some bad things in there. But they were in love."

"Fred and I are in love," Gloria said. "This is not love, it can't be. Two men can't be in love. They might love each other, they might be very close friends—like you and me. We've always been very close friends. We love each other, but we aren't in love. Our fathers had some twisted, sexualized friendship, but two men can't be in love."

"Some of them sure sound like love letters."

"It's not how God made us! Two men can't be in love!"

"It appears to be how God made our fathers. And Isaac."

"God does not make mistakes! Male and female, God created us. That's the only pairing before the fall."

"That's the only people before the fall."

"Don't go twisting things."

"Just stating facts."

"The fact, Cathy, is that God demands obedience. Our fathers and my son rebelled. Those are the facts, the sad sinful facts."

"You say that like being gay is the only way a person can rebel."

"Being homosexual is only one way we can rebel. Stop playing games."

"Gloria . . ." Cathy didn't say anything more. Gloria recognized the silence. Cathy was waiting for Gloria to see how she was in the wrong. Gloria was not having it.

"God demands obedience," she said again, more quietly.

"Doesn't God want us to honor our parents and love our children?"

Gloria lifted her head, eyes wild. "Are you accusing me of not loving my son?"

"Do you love Isaac?"

"Do I love Isaac? The hours I've spent on my knees for that boy? The hours pleading on his behalf before our Father in heaven? The fear I live in daily, the dread for his soul? Do I love Isaac? I've never prayed so hard for anyone in my whole life."

"What if he doesn't needs your prayers?" Cathy asked. "What if what he needs is your love?"

"Oh Cathy, and what does that mean?"

"I mean, it's easy to pray for someone, but do you love him enough to let him come home?"

"You know good and well he can come home anytime he's willing."

"With his—friend?"

"You mean his 'lover?'"

"Yes. His lover."

"I am not going to let him bring in this other man and let them sleep together under my roof like it isn't a sin. That all but makes me an accomplice."

"Maybe so," Cathy said and slumped back into the couch. "I just sounds like there are some rigid conditions on your love."

"I'm not playing word games with you. You're trying to trap me into saying something I don't believe."

"All I know is, I've watched Isaac grow up and I love him practically like he was one of my own. I grew up with your father and loved him like he was a second dad.

Come to find out, both of them have the same fault. Honestly, Gloria, I don't know how I feel about the gay lifestyle and all that. I just know I loved Uncle Cary and I love Isaac. I couldn't condemn either one for this offense."

"You've never been as strong in the Lord as you might be—"

Cathy interrupted. "And I've had to ask myself these last couple of weeks—in regard to our fathers, especially—I had to look at my devotion to both of those men and I have to ask, 'Do I love them more than God does? Is my love greater than God's? If I forgive them without their repentance, am I more forgiving than God?' And I thought, that sounds awfully arrogant, to say I could be more loving or more forgiving than God."

Gloria heard her friend and knew she'd just been called arrogant. She felt a rage rising and it made her head swim. She turned away, toward the kitchen.

"I need another drink of water," she said.

August 27, 1971

Dear John,

Sorry I couldn't talk much last night. Gloria came in and she wouldn't leave. I'm even sorrier I sent that note, but I'm glad I got to tell you about it before Gloria came in. Crazy. I didn't leave a note for my wife and daughter, but I sent one to you.

My head wasn't right. Maybe it still isn't.

John, I don't know what to do about all this. But I don't want to hurt Gloria and Phyllis. Or you.

I was going to crash my car. I guess I wanted it to look like an accident. I guess I trusted you with the truth. I realize now what a burden that would have been on you. I'm sorry for that, too.

I had the spot picked out. I was on my way there. I even sped up as I approached it. But then I slowed down and stopped. I realized what I was doing. I "came to myself" as they say. I laughed and cried in my car. I was so ridiculous and so sad. I was going to kill myself so I would stop loving you the way I do. I was going to kill myself because I didn't want to go to hell for loving you. Then I didn't want to go to hell for killing myself.

Once I realized I was going to hell either way, I drove home. I started another letter to you, but burned it. I don't know what to say or do. I'm sorry I wrote that note. I'm glad I called before you got it, but I'm sorry you had to know about this at all. I'm sorry to worry you. Tonight, I'm less sorry that I love you. I look at Phyllis and Gloria and what good people they are, how devout and all. I want to be like them. I want to be like them and love you. I don't know if that's possible. God help me, I want to do both.

No more suicide notes. That's all I know right now. I don't want to hurt Phyllis or Gloria or you. It seems like whatever I do I'm hurting someone. I'm just going to learn to live with it. The hurt, I mean. The hurt of cheating on Phyllis with you is nothing compared to the hurt of leaving you. That's selfish, isn't it? I wish I loved Phyllis more. I mean, I do love her. I don't want to ever leave her and I don't like keeping secrets from her. I think about you, though. All the time. More even than when I first dated Phyllis, when we were newlyweds or anytime in our romance. What does this mean? How can this be? I love you more than my wife.

Staying with Phyllis feels unfaithful to you, sometimes. That's how crazy all this is. I'm sometimes sorry you have to take a backseat to my marriage.

I guess you know what I mean. You're not talking about leaving Maddie or anything, so maybe you know what I mean.

What else to say? Thank you. I guess that's all. Just, thank you.

-Cary

9-3-71

Dear Cary,

I read your last few letters, I don't know, 20 times. I guess I'm just now understanding how much all this is bothering you. I guess I've been the thoughtless one.

On about the umpteenth read through, I started laughing. The answer is in your letter. We should stay together for our families! We can't break up because it would upset the strange little family we've created. It would upset our wives, it would devastate our daughters. Think of the children! We must work this out for the sake of the children! Ha!

Cary Cary Cary, you think too much! I love you for it and I want to pinch your head off your shoulders so you stop for a minute! You make my head hurt!

Okay, I'm not so smart, and maybe I don't think enough. But you want me to think, I'll think. Here's what I think.

Is it wrong that we're having this affair? I told you before I don't consider it cheating on Maddie because you're not the "other woman." But entertaining, for the moment, the idea that it is wrong—well I'll counter that there's something bigger wrong here. I've seen a few news stories, about some riots in fag bars and what have you. They're starting a revolution and who knows? One day maybe men like us won't have to get married just because we're supposed to. All those radical kids on the college campus—maybe they're right, maybe it's the whole damn system that needs changing. There's this system that requires men to find a woman and a woman a man and they're supposed to create families and all that. We did that, we're part of that system.

But the system isn't working for us, not entirely. What if we'd met before we got married? Or what if we hadn't felt like we were supposed to get married? Or what if we'd been allowed to think about loving another man? All that instead of stumbling upon each other in surprise? Would that have been better?

Maybe. Maybe not. I guess we'll never know. What I know is that we are here now, in this system. It's not perfect and maybe it's not even good.

But I just can't think of our time together as bad. If feelings mean anything at all, the way I feel about you means we have something good.

I wish you could feel that, too. That you can't, in my humble opinion, is <u>bad.</u>

I still love you. Thinking too much and all.

Truly yours,
John

p.s. I guess I'm kind of ignoring the suicide note. I don't know how to respond to it, except with my dumb jokes. You know how serious my jokes are, right? Maybe what I've written isn't serious enough. This is a serious as I'm going to get: I still shake when I think about you killing yourself. I'm angry, I'm grief-stricken. I'm simply shaken by it, by the thought of the world without you and that you'd leave the world because I love you. If you take anything I say seriously, take this to the bank: I would never get over losing you. Never. You left me for a job. Don't leave me any other way. Not intentionally. Got it?

Okay, I can't resist this, but you know me, you know how to read it. You know that I sometimes mean my jokes, right? So I'm going to say this in full rage and in full love: Send me another suicide note and I'll kill you! Ha!

September 15, 1971

Dear John,

You make me laugh. I'm morose and suicidal and you can still make me laugh.

I want to see you. I don't know how or when or where. I don't know how to explain it away so Phyllis and Gloria don't want to come along. Can we do that? Can we find a day, a Saturday, maybe, when we can meet halfway somewhere? I'm even willing to risk calling in sick one day, if you are. We could get caught that way, but only if Phyllis called the office. She never does. Or if the office called Phyllis. I've never called out sick, so I don't know about that.

I don't like lying, but I want to see you.

I want to kiss you first.

Love,

-Cary

Chapter 14

GLORIA DIDN'T GO TO THE SINK FOR water. She went straight to the kitchen table and sat down in a chair. Elbows on the table, forehead in her palms, she didn't want to cry, she didn't want to feel this rage, and she didn't want to think anymore.

"Sweet Jesus," she whispered. "Please, sweet Jesus. Please."

She couldn't bring herself to articulate, not even in her thought, what she was pleading for. She'd always believed, always been taught that once a person died, all chances for repentance and forgiveness were over. She couldn't repent for Daddy. She couldn't be sure he repented before he died. The best she could allow herself to ask was for some assurance that he had, in fact, repented. Then she regretted that prayer. If she got no sign of assurance, that created more despair. No, she said in her mind, no assurance. No assurance of heaven, no assurance of hell.

"Sweet Jesus," she whispered again. She stopped pleading and just called on the name of her Lord.

"Gloria. Honey." Cathy stood in the doorway and spoke softly. "You didn't get your water."

Gloria waved a hand above her head. "I decided against it."

Gloria felt Cathy's presence behind her, but she wouldn't turn around. Finally, Cathy said, "Would you like some tea?" Gloria sat there, wondering what, exactly, she would like. Cathy said, "I'm going to get me some tea. Want me to get you a glass, too?" Cathy moved to the cabinet where Gloria kept her glasses. Cathy was now in Gloria's peripheral vision and Cathy paused with the cabinet door open.

"Okay," Gloria said without looking up.

Cathy pulled down two glasses and went to the refrigerator behind Gloria. Gloria listened to Cathy open the freezer and heard the ice cubes clunk into the glasses. Then she heard Cathy open the refrigerator door and get the iced tea pitcher. She listened to the simple, ordinary sounds of Cathy setting the glasses down on the counter, the way the tea poured over the ice, the way the ice cracked. Cathy moved around Gloria's kitchen as comfortably as it was her own. Had Gloria brought bad news to Cathy's house, she could have done the same in Cathy's kitchen. The blessing of a lifelong friendship, Gloria thought again. Then she thought, today she brought a curse, too. She wondered which is stronger.

No, she thought. A blessing is always stronger than a curse. She believed that. She had to believe that.

"I think it's sweet how you still have this rock on your refrigerator, "Cathy said. "How old were they when they brought us these rocks?"

"Seventh grade. The summer before their eighth."

"Remember Amber's? She painted the moon. Didn't someone else do the sun?"

"The Kendrick boy, the one that was a slow learner."

"That's right. Amber and Isaac befriended him because he got picked on so badly. They had him do the sun because he just had to paint the rock yellow."

Gloria smiled wanly. "Yes. I was so proud of Isaac and Amber for including him."

"Amber's magnet fell off the rock sometimes ago. I don't know what became of it. It's nice you still have Isaac's."

"It reminds me to pray for him every time I see it."

Gloria felt Cathy's silence on that comment and was relieved when she heard Cathy moving again. Gloria lifted her head and received her tea. Cathy started to sit down but snapped her fingers and retrieved the sugar bowl from the cabinet. She set it and a spoon next to Gloria. Gloria smiled at the gesture and said, "Thank you." Cathy watched Gloria add sugar to her tea. The clink and rattle of the stirring filled the silence.

"I remember Isaac running to us when we picked them up," Gloria said. "He said, 'Look Mommy! The whole world on a stone!'"

Cathy nodded. "That's right. They had some game where they pretended they were space aliens and shrunk everything on the earth and the moon and the sun and put them on rocks."

"'Pocket planets,' they called them. They were going to do the same with the rest of the solar system." Gloria couldn't help but smile at the memory. "Of course, as a teacher, I couldn't let that go without explaining that the sun and moon were not planets and therefore couldn't accurately be called pocket planets."

"Oh, I can still see Isaac's eyes roll all the way to the back of his head!"

"That was about the time he started doing that."

"Puberty!" Cathy said. "Came too soon."

"Lasted too long," Gloria said, completing her part of the familiar joke between them.

Gloria sipped her tea through her smile and then grew somber.

"How many times I look at that rock and hear his changing voice. 'The whole world on a stone!' It's like he was showing me just how hard a place the world can be."

Cathy's, mouth fell into a brief frown before she took a sip of her tea.

9-22-71

Dear Cary,

You make me speechless again. Nearly.

You want to see me. Will I sound sappy if I tell you I cried when I read that? If so, I didn't. Ha!

But Cary, you lack imagination. I can't manage a whole weekend anytime soon, but a Saturday . . . <u>maybe.</u>

I found a camp grounds between us and I called them. They're booked for the fall anyway, but the guy said we could come take a look at the place before talking about spring dates. They're sending me a brochure and I have them sending one to you, too. (To your house address! All above board!)

One Saturday, we meet up there, tour the camp in the morning, and the afternoon is ours. (I'm working on the details for that, too.)

What do you say?

When I got your letter, it was all I could do to not get in the car and start driving.

I think your letter even smelled like you, which made it even harder. (Pun intended! Ha!)

Love,

John

p.s. I'm going to hold you to your promise to kiss me first. <u>Probably.</u> Ha!

October 6, 1971

Dear John,

Thank you for setting up the trip to the camp ground. You're right. I lack imagination. That's why I need you. One reason, anyway.

I couldn't say anything on the phone tonight. I couldn't get Phyllis and Gloria to both leave the room at the same time.

Gloria is always praying. I admire her for that. I guess I was always afraid to pray so much. What if God answered? What if He sent fire down on me? I know you're laughing now. But I'm serious.

Ever since that time with my car, you know when I didn't crash it, I've been praying. A lot. Mostly in my car, before and after work. Praying for some sign, I guess. Some hint that we—God and me—were okay. And, yes, that you and I were okay.

Part of me had decided to enjoy our relationship, even if I ended up in hell. To not love you meant I didn't want to live. I failed at suicide for fear of hell. Fear of hell isn't keeping me from loving you.

I don't know if this makes sense. I think maybe it doesn't.

But after only a few weeks, I think I have my sign.

Someone is retiring back in the old office. I'm perfect for the job. It's my natural next step in the company. It's even a promotion and raise. When I heard of it, I went and talked to my boss about it. He said my name had already been mentioned. He asked if I would willing to go through the trouble of another transfer.

107

I hope I didn't appear too anxious when I said I would.

Nothing is settled. There are things they have to get lined up. It could fall through. I haven't told Phyllis and Gloria about it.

But I had to tell you. I'm praying about this. For this. Maybe you could, too.

See you in two weeks.

With love,
-Cary

10-11-71

Dear Cary,

YES! YES! YES!

I'm shaking. I'm actually shaking. I may cry.

I don't know how we'll get through that camp tour. I'll be shaking the whole time I'm next to you.

This has to come through. It would be too cruel if it didn't.

Do what you what you have to. Tell me who to bribe— I'll find the money!

Praying, pleading, all that and more.

See you next weekend.

Love,

John

p.s. I don't suppose the family with the hyena children have missed any payments on the house. I told you to rent, not sell!

10-24-71

Dear Cary,

Wow. Man. When you decide to kiss first, you <u>kiss first!</u> I know you don't like to get too graphic on paper, so I'll keep my thoughts to myself.

Except this one: <u>WOW!</u>

Ha!

Any word?

I'm driving around the neighborhood, looking for houses for sale. If you can't live next door, I'm determined to find something for you in the neighborhood.

It's so hard not to call every night and ask if you've heard anything.

You'll call when you do, right?

Love,

John

p.s. Oh yeah, that camp was nice, wasn't it? The whole 15 minutes we were there! Ha!

November 17, 1971

Dear John,

Things move slowly. The upcoming holidays won't help. Still I keep being told it looks good. Then they say, "The only thing that would stop it is _____"

They fill in the blank with a list of things. Most of the things are out of my control.

I've told Phyllis and Gloria about it. Gloria wanted to know about the holidays and your family. I was hoping we'd be moving back for Christmas. I guess that was a lot of wishful thinking. It would be a cleaner break for Gloria to transfer schools at the Christmas break. Nothing is that clean and easy, I guess.

So, what about the holidays? Your place for New Year's? I keep my hopes up that I'll know by then and we can look at homes. I guess we'll see.

Phyllis is excited about moving back. Gloria, too, but I can tell she was just getting used to the idea of being here long term. You know, graduating with some new friends. But she says Cathy is still her best friend. I think its all okay.

I'm on pins and needles.

With love,
-Cary

12-3-71

Dear Cary,

It's after midnight here. I can't sleep. Cathy had a hard time going to bed, too, but she's finally turned out her light and I think she's asleep. Even Maddie was kind of keyed up for a while, but you know her. She's the most practical of all of us. She went to bed first and is fast asleep.

After we finally hung up the phone, Cathy and I jumped up and down and screamed a little bit. No joke. Maddie laughed at us, but you could tell she's excited you're all moving back.

If I wouldn't wake up Maddie and Cathy, I'd scream again right now.

So it won't be before Christmas. This is still an early Christmas gift. And whenever you get here, it'll be another gift.

And if it seemed like an impetuous offer, Maddie and I talked more about it and we're really agreed. If it can be worked out with the schools, of course Gloria can come live with us until you get everything settled. She's like the daughter who went away to boarding school or something. Of course, she's welcome here. She's welcome home. And it's got to be easier to move her here at the Christmas break than to move midstream in the new semester, right? If the school district requires it, Phyllis can stay here, too. You know, whatever we can do to help.

It's like a bad dream is ending. You were away, and now you're coming back!

When I'm not shouting, I'm crying. Happy tears, though. Happy, happy tears!

I could write to you all night, I think, if I could think of something else to write. All I have to say is you're coming back! You're coming back! You're coming back! Over and over.

No joke, that's all that's on my mind.

Maybe I'll try to go to bed again. Maybe I'll dream about you. Happy dreams!

Love,
John

December 15, 1971

Dear John,

We'll look into the rules at the school district. Gloria seems up for it. She's had a couple of somber moments. She's made a few friends here. She has the most mixed emotions about the news. I think Phyllis is as excited as I am. She really never found a place to fit in here.

Of course, it won't be the same as before. We can't move back into our old house and tear down the fence between our backyards. And I'm sorry about all that. I truly am.

But I think I'll be better. I mean I am more at peace about us. About you and me. And you know, it's a peace I think God gave me. I really do. I guess I can tell you this.

Gloria's been real involved with her church youth group here. She says her walk with the Lord has gotten stronger here. I think she'll miss the youth group. If she could have Cathy in the group, she'd rather stay, I think.

Anyway, she pushed me to join a men's breakfast Bible study. They meet once a week before work at this diner. One morning, a few weeks ago already, the pastor was leading a study on David. The pastor was talking about how David was a great king and a great man of God. He sort of mentioned his friendship with Jonathan, just in passing. David and Jonathan's friendship didn't sit well with Jonathan's father, Saul.

I'd finished my breakfast and was flipping around in my Bible. Just skimming around the pages where Pastor had been reading. I found a place where it said David and

114

Jonathan kissed. Then I saw a place where it said, I think, David said Jonathan's love was better than a woman's.

I guess I was too quiet, too long. Pastor asked me what I was reading. I showed him. I said I had a friend like Jonathan. I said I had to leave my friend when I moved. I said I missed him.

I didn't really get emotional, but I think I made a couple of the men uncomfortable. Pastor said something about the importance of friendships. Something about that Bible study group was a place to make new friends.

It was that morning that I realized I could be okay with us. About you and me. It was that day that I started looking for openings in my old office. That it all happened so quickly after that Bible study feels like God leading. You can laugh at me if you want. That's what it feels like.

I wonder what it would be like to have met you before Phyllis. Maybe that's pointless wondering. I'd never leave her, certainly not my Gloria. I'd never want to hurt them.

I can only say I'm sorry I ever hurt you. I'm sorry I'm only going to be able to go a certain distance for you. With you.

But I am thankful for you and your love. It's better than the love of women.

With Love,

-Cary

P.S. I may not get another letter written before, so Merry Christmas. I'm sure we'll talk before then.

Christmas Day

Dear Cary,

It's been a big day here. All the grandparents here, Cathy excited about that. Lots of food, plenty of presents.

Everyone has settled down now, in bed. Here I am, in my pajamas, at the kitchen table, writing to you. Sending you Christmas Day greetings.

I guess we won't have much need for our p.o. boxes soon. I'll be glad to have you a few minutes away instead of a letter away. I'll be glad to see you more often. I'll be glad to have these months behind us.

These were hard months, Cary. For me, anyway. Really hard. I never planned to crash my car, though, so I guess they were worse for you. For all the ways I maybe contributed to your planning that, I'm sorry. I thank God you didn't. And if you've found peace and are able to come back here, come back to me, well, what else could I want for Christmas?

I know we'll never know all the "what ifs" about our lives. I can't think of any way I'd feel fair leaving Maggie and Cathy. I've even thought that if we have to live in this system of things, we're lucky to understand each other in this. Yeah, divorce doesn't make sense. We have our strange little family—two girls, four parents! It seems to be good as it is. I'm just thankful for you, for however we can be together, whenever we can be together.

It's a merry Christmas. I hope it's our last one apart.

Love,
John (athan)
(Ha!)

February 6, 1972

Dear John,

The house is empty, the movers are loaded. I have to turn over the keys to the real estate agent in the morning. Then I have to stop by the office for some final business there.

It's ridiculous to write to you. I'll see you tomorrow. I just saw you two days ago.

I'm just writing to put words on paper.

I'm here alone, in a motel room. Of course I'm thinking of you. It's too late to call, so I'm writing, one last note from this city.

I guess that's something else I need to do tomorrow. Stop by the post office and close out my box rental.

I guess after you get this letter, you can do the same.

Thank you for these letters. They've changed my life. They even saved my life. I might still wish things could be different, but I can't imagine them any other way. Thank you. That's why I'm writing. To say thank you.

And to say one other thing. I'm coming back to you thankful to God for you. I couldn't say that when I moved here. Now I can hardly think anything else.

I'm sitting here staring at the paper. I don't want to end this letter. I guess there's nothing else to say for now.

Thank you. I'm thankful for you.

I promise to never leave you again.

With Love, Faithfully,
-Cary

Chapter 15

GLORIA RAN HER HANDS over the smooth Formica of the table. "The last meal Daddy had in this house was at this table. It was just a lunch, as informal as you and me here." She wiped at a sweat ring, made by her tea glass. "Isaac was here, too, home from Bible College. He was taking a class on the Old Testament or Genesis or something like that. The other students kept joking about sacrificing him, taking him up on a hill somewhere and seeing if God would speak to stop them, too. He said how tired he was of it, how it verged on blasphemy. Daddy basically told him to lighten up." Gloria's shoulders gave a small shake as she suppressed a laugh. "Daddy said to remember that Isaac meant laughter that he should just laugh along. Isaac answered that Sarah laughed out of joy, not mockery. And Daddy said, 'Like Sarah, we didn't think our Isaac could be born. What a shame for someone born in such joy to turn out to be such a sourpuss.' I nearly burst trying not to laugh. My serious father, lecturing my serious son to lighten up. I thought, they're so alike."

Cathy let that thought float in the air, delicate as a soap bubble.

"I just said that maybe Uncle John should go to that Bible College and show those kids a thing or two about mockery."

Cathy laughed. "Oh, Daddy would have enjoyed that!"

"Daddy laughed at that, too. He said that wouldn't be fun for those poor college kids. Isaac rolled his eyes but then he had to smile. Uncle John made Isaac a little crazy but he still loved him." Gloria took a sip of her tea. "But of course, Isaac is so much like his grandpa."

Gloria saw her friend's smile fade. She felt Cathy watching her closely.

"It's all tainted, Cathy Cat."

"No."

"That last lunch with Daddy and Isaac, a cherished memory, and now it's tainted. All my observations of their similarities, so innocent, hopeful, even. Since Isaac declared himself a homosexual, I kept thinking, maybe he'll still grow into a man like Daddy, that good, wonderful family man!" Gloria stood up suddenly and Cathy jumped. Gloria paced.

"How? How does this happen, Cathy? Why did they have to have that affair? Why did they leave those letters? What the hell were they thinking?"

Gloria stopped in front of the refrigerator, startled by her own use of the word "hell." She wildly grabbed at Isaac's rock magnet. With a sound like a grunt and a cry, she threw it without aim. Cathy recoiled. It hit the window over the sink and bounced and clattered in the stainless steel drain. Gloria's grocery list lay at her feet. A single crack ran across the window pane.

"Gloria."

Gloria began to cry again. "Look at that, Cathy. All my rage isn't even enough to throw a rock through a

119

window." Gloria covered her face with her hands, standing in her kitchen, crying.

Cathy stood up and went to the sink. She picked up the rock and looked at the window. "It's enough to make a good crack," she said. She picked up the grocery list from the floor and put it and the stone back on the refrigerator. She stood behind her crying friend and put her arms around Gloria's shoulders. Cathy whispered in Gloria's ears. "Maybe it's just that the world isn't as hard as you make it out to be."

Gloria turned around and clung to her friend, sobbed into Cathy's shoulder.

"Shh," Cathy said, stroking Gloria's hair. "Shh. It's okay, Glory Glory. It's going to be okay."

November 1, 2009

My dear Little Girl,

I'm leaving you this bundle of letters. Back when Cary learned he was dying, he brought his half to me and he wanted us to burn them together. I begged him to let me keep them, for something to hold onto after he was gone. I can't tell you how many times I've read them since he died. I imagine I'll read them a few more times before I die. I wish there were more of them. We only wrote to each other those months while he and Phyllis and Gloria had moved away back in 1970. I'm sure you remember that.

Cary wanted me to burn them eventually. Maybe you'll wish I had, too. Maybe they'll be upsetting to you and Gloria, but they'll explain a few things.

For you, I hope you'll have more of an understanding about why your mother and I divorced. Maddie knew about me and Cary for the last few years of our marriage but she put up with it, God love her. I think she didn't want to break up the ol' gang. For so long it was John and Maddie and Cary and Phyllis. And of course, we all raised you and Gloria almost like you were sisters, all one family.

But after Phyllis died, well, the gang was broken up, I guess. She didn't want to embarrass anyone and she wasn't ugly or vindictive about it. I'll always love her for that. But, as she put it, with Phyllis gone, she was the third wheel. She thought Cary and I should have some years together, just the two of us. I think she expected us to move in together and honestly, I wanted to. Cary couldn't bring himself to be anywhere near that open. The only nights we ever spent together were when we traveled. Even that made him nervous. Made me crazy, especially as I saw other male couples being more open over the years. If I hadn't loved him so much, I never would have put up with it.

Anyway, I'm glad Maddie found her Gerry. She deserved to have someone who loves her in a way I never could.

Now, for Gloria, well, you know she's like a second daughter to me. All one big family, right? I'm a coward. I wanted to say something to her when her troubles with Isaac started. Maybe I should have. I wonder what Cary would have said, had he lived long enough. It's up to you if you show Gloria these letters, but I hope you do. I want her to know how much her father loved her, but that he loved me, too. I love her, and I loved her father. I don't know how to explain it better than that. If God thinks it's wrong, then He'll have to explain it better than that. Maybe then I'll apologize for all this loving. But probably not.

Well, that's all I've got to say. The letters will have to say the rest. I'm sorry I wasn't brave enough to tell you this sooner. I'm sure you'll have questions. Well, not all questions are answered. I hope it helps that, without question, Cary and I both loved our daughters.

All my love,
Daddy

Chapter 16

GLORIA LET CATHY GUIDE HER back to the living room. The two women sat on the sofa as Cathy cradled Gloria. They didn't speak.

This blessing, Gloria thought, this lifelong friendship. How many times had they been here, one cradling the other, offering comfort, sharing grief. As girls, death of pets gave way to deaths of grandparents, broken toys gave way to broken hearts. As women, there were deaths of parents, infidelity, the news there would be no more children after Daniel.

Except there was Isaac, one more son who brought laughter and then more tears.

Things aren't what they seem, Gloria thought. Maybe this friendship isn't real, either. Maybe her parents were never married, maybe Fred was never faithful, and maybe she wasn't a good daughter, wife, teacher, and mother.

How could she tell?

Daddy and Uncle John. Their affection for each other was real and somehow it turned sinful. How long? How long before they turned to a sinful relationship? How long did it last? They were in their mid-to-late thirties when they met, grown men who had started families. Old enough to know better.

Momma and Aunt Maddie were friends, too, but Gloria always sensed it was different for them. They loved each other, but it was different. It never crossed a line to sinful behavior. That Gloria knew of.

Everything was in doubt. Gloria wondered if anything could possibly be true. Was she the only one who remained faithful, who counted faithfulness as an inviolable standard?

She was ashamed of the thought. Cathy. Cathy was always faithful, at least to people. She didn't leave Charles when she had every reason to. In honesty, Gloria might have drifted from the friendship during her high school year and a half away, or during college. There were opportunities for Gloria to just let the friendship drop during the courtship of husbands and marriages. But Cathy made the effort. She remained a faithful friend.

"You know, Cathy Cat," Gloria said softly, "I never wanted to be the type of woman who cried when she was angry."

"Oh, Glory." Cathy was silent for a moment. "Name it, sweetie. Tell me everything you're mad about."

Gloria smiled. Ever since she and Charles had their troubles and went to counseling, Cathy sometimes sounded like a counselor, too. Gloria played along.

"I'm mad at Daddy and Uncle John for cheating on our mothers," Gloria said. "I'm mad they had a homosexual affair. I'm mad they endangered their immortal souls that way. I'm mad at you for telling me about it. I'm mad at the devil for tempting people with homosexual lusts. I'm mad at Daddy and Uncle John for falling into the temptation. May as well throw in Isaac, too. I'm mad at you for telling

Isaac about Uncle John and Daddy. I'm mad Momma and Daddy—." Gloria paused. "I'm mad there's not a thing I can do about any of it."

After a long silence, Cathy said, "That's a lot of mad."

Gloria said, "You asked."

Cathy said, "You said you were mad at me twice."

Gloria said, "Don't take it personally."

Cathy laughed and pushed Gloria to sit upright and Gloria laughed, too, if only a little. Laughing with Cathy, the bedrock beneath the sand.

"Sweetie, are you going to be okay?" Cathy asked.

"Oh, eventually. I guess."

"Will you eventually forgive me for telling you all this?"

Gloria ran her fingers through her hair. "Eventually. I guess you were right to tell me. I just have to think on it a while."

"Of course. I'm still processing it, too."

"All this homosexuality. The devil's working overtime on it."

"I think what these letters mean is it's always been there, it just used to be hidden away."

"Of course we've always had sin. We just used to be ashamed of it. People used to not go around in parades and festivals, flaunting their sin."

"Maybe so," Cathy sighed. "But really, don't you think how Isaac is living has a little more integrity than the way our fathers lived? I mean, our poor moms."

Gloria closed her eyes and dropped her head. "I don't think I'm up for a debate about levels of integrity while rebelling against how God made us."

"Okay," Cathy said. "Okay. Well, if you're okay, I'm going to head home. I imagine you want some time to yourself before Fred gets home."

"I do. I do." Gloria turned to Cathy. "You haven't told Charles anything about this?"

"Not yet. I'm working up to it." Cathy smiled. "All he knows is that I've been going through Daddy's things and that I've been a little moody about it. He hasn't questioned it and I haven't explained."

"I don't think I'll be ready to talk about it with Fred tonight. Or it might just spill out."

Cathy nodded, smiling. "You do it when you need to. Or when you think Fred is ready to hear it."

"He'll be better about it than I was this afternoon. I mean, he's the one who's always telling me to lighten up on Isaac. I've always thought I was light on Isaac."

"Yes, Glory Glory, we all know you think you've laid a light hand on Isaac."

Gloria felt her defenses rise and then pushed them away. "I'm just trying to be faithful to my Father in heaven."

"I think Isaac is, too."

"It doesn't look like it from where I sit."

"Then find another seat."

"Cathy, I just can't be flip with my son's soul."

"And you can't control everything he does."

"Are you calling me a controlling mother?"

"That isn't what I was getting at, but now that you bring it up—"

"Stop right there, Cathy Cat." Gloria put a hand up to Cathy's face. Gloria laughed in spite of herself.

Cathy took hold of Gloria's hand and pulled it down. She held onto Gloria's hands with both of hers.

"What I was getting at," Cathy said, "is that being faithful to your Father in heaven doesn't mean you can't also be faithful to your son on earth. I mean, what does faithfulness mean if you distance yourself when something goes wrong?"

Gloria sat still, letting her faithful friend hold her hand.

"Cathy Cat, you've always lived faithful to all of us in your life. Sometimes I've wondered how you did it. I've even questioned it." Gloria squeezed Cathy's fingers. "Maybe I should pay more attention."

Cathy shook her head. "I don't know about all that. I do know it's time I get a move on. You're sure you're okay?"

Gloria let go of Cathy's hands and nodded. "I'll be fine. I just want some time before Fred gets home." She glanced at the clock on the wall. "I only have about three hours to work through all this."

Both women laughed. Cathy stood up and pulled Gloria up with her. Cathy gave Gloria a strong embrace and then headed to the front door. "Well, don't be disappointed if you don't get it all worked through today."

Gloria followed Cathy to the door. "You mean I might have to think about this tomorrow?"

"You might."

Cathy opened the door and stood in the doorway as Gloria said, "Then I might have to talk some tomorrow."

127

"I'll leave my cell on," Cathy said and she blew Gloria a kiss. "Bye-bye, Glory Glory."

"Goodbye, Cathy Cat."

With a click of the door, Gloria was alone. She turned around and looked at her living room. It looked the same. It only felt like everything had changed.

She picked up the stack of letters. She thought about reading them right then, but instead stuffed them toward the back of a drawer in the small desk in the corner of the living room.

She looked at her photo wall. She tried to not feel differently about them, tried not to see them differently.

She turned to go to the kitchen but stopped. She wasn't ready to look at that cracked window pane. She wondered what she would tell Fred about that. That window was definitely different this afternoon, different from this morning. She decided to stay a few more minutes in the living room, where everything still looked the same.

She thought of the One who remained the same forever. She walked over to the sofa, pulled up a cushion, and tossed it to the floor. She kneeled down and began to pray.

She prayed for—*about* her parents, who were beyond her intercessions now, but she could still talk to the Lord about them, how she loved them, was thankful for them, how she missed them, how she suddenly didn't understand their lives. She prayed for Isaac, still within reach of her intercessions. She prayed he would turn from his rebellion and she prayed to be a faithful mother all the same. She prayed for comfort, understanding, and peace of mind.

Most of all, she prayed, "Make me faithful. Lord Jesus, I want to be faithful. To Fred, to Cathy, to Isaac and Daniel, yes, Lord to all of them but most of all to you. I just want to be faithful to you, Lord Jesus. Find me faithful to your perfect will. Jesus, make me faithful. I just want to be faithful."

Made in United States
North Haven, CT
09 August 2022

22461837R00075